NEW TALES FOR OLD

NEW TALES FOR OLD

Robin Nuruddin Hood,
Dracula, Otello, Oisin
and other stories

Abdassamad Clarke

By: Abdassamad Clarke
Short stories edited by: Abd al-Baseer Ojembarrena

British Library Cataloguing in Publication Data

Clarke, Abdassamad
New Tales For Old
I. Title

ISBN 978-1-943277-26-1

CONTENTS

SHORT STORIES   1

AND WHY NOT?   3

ROBIN NURUDDIN HOOD   12

DRACULA   24

BILLY THE KID   47

OTELLO AND DESDEMONA   56

OISIN SHEATHES HIS SWORD   66

   Oisin and Niamh   66

   Oisin and a Cleric   70

   Oisin Waits Even Now   82

THE GREATEST NAME OF ALLAH   89

POETRY   97

GOD IS DEAD   99

THE COLT   105

SHORT STORIES

AND WHY NOT?

That question often occurred to her, but only momentarily in the darkest recesses of what she liked to think of as her heart. What was it that she plotted so secretly alone in the night? It was not so much a plot as a continual movement of her thinking. It does not even matter so much what it was, but only that she endlessly reverted to that thought, that it came naturally to her, that everything she saw or read or listened to, refuelled this one inner reflection. In that, one might call it her religion because it absorbed her, body, mind and soul.

Alex, her eldest son, who would come visiting sometimes with his wife, never knew about these inward movements of his mother's consciousness. How could he when she was his mother? He had not yet learnt to see her as independent from him, a being, with her own destiny. She was still his mother, and in that Elizabeth acquiesced, if somewhat reluctantly. But to the extent that Alex lived so far away and came to visit less frequently over the years, Elizabeth came more and more to be herself and less and less his mother. Alex never knew this, selfish young man that he was, because he never experienced her in any other way than as 'mum'.

And Rosemary had always been a difficult child, jealous

at the affection Alex and Elizabeth had shared and at what Alex was allowed to get away with. Yet motherhood had taught her something of what her own mother had had to endure. Alex and Maureen, who were without children as yet, could not experience that. Maureen, on the other hand, and against his and her will, as they both thought, had found herself drawn into mothering Alex.

Perhaps now the light of understanding is dawning. This is going to be one of those deep and penetrating pictures of family life, shot through with Jungian or Freudian insights into its mechanisms.

There is no doubt that all of these things take place in most family lives. How many young men do not end up in some way marrying their mothers? Just look at the faces of defeat on the streets and how the young are so quickly transformed by life, marriages and above all parenthood into caricatures of human beings, all the freshnesss washed from their hearts and their eyes.

How easily we settle down to defeat, to the realistic view of existence. Indeed Elizabeth had almost done so. She still remembered the arguments with her own mother when she had been an idealistic girl.

"But life's not like that!" her career-minded mother had argued vehemently, "It's not black and white. Things are not so clear, there are all sorts of shades of grey." Elizabeth had held herself back in obstinate refusal of this view, yet with nothing, no answer to it, but a deep conviction that it was deeply wrong. Then marriage had happened to her and with it children and the loss of the immediate chance to realise the passionate vision of her adolescence, a vision which adhered to her from far back in her radiant childhood, that timeless age when one sees clearly.

Somewhere within this now middle-aged lady she had always protected a movement of her intellect, which she had never been able to express. Thus it was protected from being subsumed under philosophy or some other category of man's thinking. Things that are categorised are easily dealt with. The arguments are worn out. No need to think about that because so-and-so has already done so. "Don't you realise that is the position of the neo-Platonists?" Thought is something for the great and the famous, for professionals. The rest of us are lucky that we live in a literate society and can humbly sit at the bottom of the pages of their books and try and digest their thinking. But do not be so arrogant as to try and think for yourself!

Elizabeth was wont to think thoughts that frightened her. Despite being widely read she knew of nobody that had thought her thoughts. If she had thought in only one category she might have learnt that, "Dirac said that, or Plotinus, Ibn al-Arabi or Ayer." Then she might have been able to stop thinking them and read their books instead. The few times she mentioned it to her husband he pooh-poohed it. Thinkers are famous people, great people. They are not just your wife of twenty-five years. And so she had become silent and got on with the porridge.

Nor were her thoughts abstruse, in fact she could

not understand why no-one else seemed to be thinking them. Television it was had opened her eyes. She had struggled against the inevitability of sitting down in front of the goggle-box, she had fought her man, she had warred on the children but in the end the box had won and they had all tuned in to the mindlessness which they all knew it to be. Alex had been the worst, she thought, with his criminal shoot-outs and his sneaking down at night to watch the semi-pornographic and titillating programming allowed at adult hours. Like many mothers she had known an awful lot more about her children's secret lives than she cared to admit but concealed it under motherly concern. Fifteen had been a difficult age for her and it had been difficult enough for Alex.

Caught up in the mindlessness of family life in front of the hypnotic box, she had refused to submit to its charms, which in reality were few enough. She submitted it, in its turn, to a scrutiny so intense that she was inadvertently to burst through to an entirely different reality altogether and be bathed in an overflow of light and love that had transformed her. It was that experience which had brought her oh-so slowly but inexorably to the "Why not?" question and it was a thought unlike any of the others she had ever thought. It was not some secret undercurrent in a dark cavernous place of her being, but the entire river about to surface from underneath the ground and run beneath the sky, be it sunny or obscured.

It was the dots that did it. The little electronics that she had picked up, from her son's studies and her own education had told her about the cathode ray tube and how it builds up images by creating thousands of dots every second in rows across the screen. "But I don't see it like that," she thought, and it began to absorb her in a puzzled kind of way. This was Coronation Street, mind you, or was it another one of those utterly indistinguishable soaps? She was very aware of losing consciousness of her surroundings and becoming enmeshed in the drama before her, whether the crisis in the Middle East or in Neighbours. More shockingly, when she entered the room where her children or her husband were watching something not to her favour, and there was little that she really watched out of interest, was the feeling that something was desperately wrong. These idiot faces laughing at the antics of some moron or caught up in the working-out of some pathetic American cop drama, were extremely disturbing.

"And it's all dots! Just dots!" she thought and resolved then to try to see it as it is, to see the dots. That was not difficult because despite the stupid programmes' almost hypnotic control over them, she could plainly see the lines and their little coloured points across the screen and there was a sense of newness and discovery when this box was revealed ever so slightly as a deception.

"And if," she had thought, "My brain fleshes out those dots into a moving drama that can have me on the edge of my seat or in tears, perhaps then my brain is doing the same all the time while I am unawares, perhaps so called reality is just dots."

Briefly she had mentioned it to her apparently oh-too-bright son Alex when he visited once and he had told her rather condescendingly about sub-atomic particle physics as it stood at that particular moment. It did not seem to penetrate his skull, though, that he was made of all those particles and vortices of energy and so she came to distrust a knowledge that left the knower so disconnected and her link to her son was further weakened and a distance grew where there had been maternal closeness.

He was puzzled by that for it was his prerogative to kick against her demanding maternal instinct and she had left him nothing to kick against at all. She had queried her own behaviour very much and doubted herself up until that glorious moment when she had seen. The whole picture had come into focus in a way that she had never thought possible at all, strangely enough when her children had gathered in her home for the annual mid-winter family get-together.

Tight with frustration at the passing of her life, and her family's lives, uselessly, irritated beyond bearing at the replay of a mindless movie, which yet despite the resistance of her awakening intellect held her hypnotised, she focused the television and its dots. This strange box with its glittering screen and drifting in and out of focus the characters who were just made of these dots, funny little coloured dots, and her family around her mindless of each other, perhaps unable to confront each other and the little dramatic interplays that they had become so used to, the snarls of irritation, the jokey familiar put-downs, the affection of those who have known each other too closely and too long, too isolatedly, the contempt which leads to familiarity. As she brought her being to ignore no thing present but bring it all into awareness, censuring nothing however barbed and painful, something happened which was more precisely a nothing. She was gone and there was only one, for just a brief nothing of time, and she was bathed in a warm compassionate light and affection that washed all over her family, the room and made the television recede to the borders of her estate.

The experience was somehow like the time when as a child she had come across, in the country, in the most unlikely place, a beautiful lawn which thoughtlessly she had stepped straight on to, only to plummet through it into the waters of the pond beneath that treacherous, oh-so-green carpet of algae. That had been an unpleasant and frightening event because she was a creature of land used to abiding in air and suddenly she was enveloped by a cold alien element, water. But this moment that happened for her was as if she were a water creature all unknown to herself, trapped on land, who on falling into the pond suddenly discovered that she was a fish out of her element. She had found her element and her true abode and although she had been returned to dry land the same moment that she had 'fallen in', as she used to put it, she now knew without any doubt what her element was and that she had not been created to be a subject of the television, imprisoned by its baleful glare, seduced by its tawdry baubles, programmed by its one-dimensional view of existence. It had merely found its proper perspective and was now a remote object in her existence, as were, unhappily, her husband and her family.

Yet she was convinced that they too were were fish out of water but knew beyond any argument that they could never rationally be brought around to that thought, that somehow they had to be pushed in the deep end, and she had not the slightest clue as to how that could be done. Indeed she now had the most urgent need to find out what was the name of the water into which she had fallen and if anyone else at all had ever been in it. Without a doubt she knew that she was a fish of those types which swim in shoals, rather than lone vicious sharks and that if she was to survive she must now be ruthless in finding her shoal.

Suddenly her life was filled with purpose, fear and longing. She understood now Stephen Dedalus in *The Portrait of the Artist as a Young Man* when he decided to leave his old haunts and his old existence, his family and native country, in order to find a new mode of life or art, needing for it silence, exile and cunning. And poor Joyce had had to settle for art, second best, but she knew that that was an option which was not open to her and that perforce she must seek a new mode of life in the ocean with gambolling mermans and mermaids and sea-nymphs rather than with the endless life of chewing the cud that the bovine people she called her family and neighbours seemed to espouse.

Ibsen's heroine slammed the door of her *Doll's House* to

great effect in the 19th century but Elizabeth left very quietly taking care not to disturb the herd in its grazing as she left. She knew that they would moo and low a great deal but that ultimately they would return to the box and to the TV dinners with just a tiny puzzlement unacknowledged in a corner of their screens. She for her part having found her ocean knew that the shoal could not be far away and so leaving behind all those once-treasured items of those who inhabit the land, to the greater puzzlement of her once-close ones, she slipped into the bracingly chilly waters of existence, thinking, "And why not?" She had no answer to that, but to her mother she sent a belated reply, "Yes, mother, life is not black and white, it is a wonderful spectrum of rainbow colours of which black, white and all the greys are just tiny parts. So, yes, why not?"

ROBIN NURUDDIN HOOD

He sprawled exhausted against the tree and let fly with his last arrow, possibly the most famous arrow ever to be loosed from bow in England.

"Where it falls there bury me," he faintly gasped so that all had to lean closer to catch the words, but then he spoke with unanticipated force, "As a Muslim, mind!" and they nodded their heads. Thus passed away one of the great men indeed of the English, Robin Nuruddin Hood, and it is my task to put right the record on the man which has been so maliciously altered.

My name is Abdullah Tuck, his Imam many a long year in the wonderful forest of Sherwood, perhaps the most beautiful mosque in the world, certainly the only one I've seen, so I have no real means of comparing to know.

The men went and found the arrow. A party have gone with shovels to dig, carrying his blessed body which is so light and sweet in death as never did I see the like of. And the abbot of my first ordaining, how heavy in comparison, how quick to rot and how glad were we to see him under the soil. But let me go back to the beginning of the story while they are away and use my scrivener's training for this one last task to tell the true story of noble Robin Hood which otherwise may never be told in truth.

'Twas while serving in far and distant lands his king, he that is called Richard the Lionheart though Cravenheart did we come to call him, that my Master Nuruddin got the name that I will call him by at that point in the narrative which suits. Robin, as then he was, went not as many a merry adventurer and freebooter for pillage, rape and spoils, but driven by a longing to see the Holy Land where the Messiah, peace be upon him, had walked upon its soil. True he also accepted, what all of us had been told from the cradle, that Mahometans were infidels, enemies of our Lord and truly worthy of extermination. Yet Robin, ever a tenderhearted being, most passionately longed for their conversion to the 'true' faith, as indeed did many a noble knight.

Yet, strange to say, a coincidence set him off on his path, on a very different footing from what he had imaged. By a marvellous chance he had cause to visit the learned Abbot of a monastery not far from the lands of his noble father. The revered old man was steeped in lore of both the ancients and the Bible; he was a reservoir of Greek knowledge, Syriac, Aramaic, Hebrew and other learning that few others of any age master. And still the old man remained strangely unsatisfied. His learning only added fuel to his desire to know more. Indeed his advancing years only seemed to lend desperation to his quest as if he was in danger of passing away while yet being within reach of his goal but not having attained it.

The aged Abbot was fair set on fire by Master Robin of Loxley's visit for he somehow recognised in him a kindred spirit, though Squire Robin neither before nor since showed any inclination to rout among manuscripts. But what sent the old man into a delirium of excitement was the knowledge that Robin, pure-hearted being that he was, went to the Holy Land as a pilgrim not as pirate or bandit. If the truth be told, most of our kinsfolk went for pillage. Naturally they spouted a great deal of Latin and dressed in crosses and the Bishops prayed very much for all concerned. But I think seeing those bloodthirsty robbers and brigands set sail, robed in the cloak of religion, blessed by mother church, I think that was the first thing in my adult life that set me a-thinking, even though in those days my liking for ale was such that I did not progress very far in thought at that point.

Robin told me about that meeting in later years.

"Squire Loxley," the old Abbot said, sizing Robin up as if judging whether to entrust him with some momentous secret, "What do you say to the Mahometans and us?"

"Why, Abbot, they are damned and we are saved, God be praised," Robin said with the cheerful certitude which he was soon to lose and yet regain though only after a sizeable period of doubt and deep thought.

"Wish that it were so simple," the Abbot replied, eyeing

Robin to judge his response to this less than orthodox remark. Robin, with his great trusting heart, was open to the Abbot's superior knowledge and so merely looked slightly puzzled.

"Wish that it were so simple," the Abbot repeated, and turned away looking for something among the piles of manuscripts laden on his old oak table. Sunlight streamed in from a beautifully blue sky with just such cloud cover as makes an English spring day so unique.

"What, dear master, do you say to the Mahometans and us?" ventured bold Robin of Loxley, inquisitively yet genially enough, so that the old Abbot after scrutinizing his open countenance found courage to address these words to Robin, words which were to transform the man forever.

"Robin," he said, "We've been lied to for hundreds of years. They follow our Lord more truly than do we."

Now that I have written those lines they seem bland enough but as Robin told them to me they hit some deep area in his bosom and try as he would he could never wrest them from his heart even in the most extreme circumstance.

Faced with some Saracen warrior in battle, Robin would be weakened by the thought, "He follows our Lord more truly than do we."

There you have the reason why he did not cut such a dashing figure in the Crusades, our Robin whose valour and chivalry were never questioned. For without doubt a man may fight with excellent weapons, he may have the best martial training in the arts of war that an Englishman could have, his company may be brave but if his heart be not in what he does he is doomed. If he does not believe in his cause he cannot win and even if he did by some accident win, his very victory would be ashen and bitter in his mouth.

Now you see what laid poor Robin at the feet of the Saracen on that fateful day, a man who was in truth not his equal in battle.

"*Aslim!*" the man said, and Robin, who had never acquired so much as a word of their lingo, merely gazed up into the marvellous light brown complexion of the man, a man he was later to learn was a true Arab of the desert. Something in his complete acquiescence must have spoken to that Arab and touched his heart, for Robin neither struggled to flee, pleaded for his life nor sought some means to regain his weapon to defend himself or at least do hurt to that Arabic man before he died. Truly the struggle within his breast as to the truth of the position of the Saracens and the Crusaders overcame him then and there.

He later told me, "At that moment I was completely surrendered to whatever my destiny was, completely at ease and reconciled to whether I should be killed, captured, imprisoned, enslaved or set free. Indeed my senses were overcome by the beauty of the day and the extraordinary visage of that fierce Saracen."

"Muslim," the Arab said and pointed to Robin, and Robin could see that, in the middle of the carnage which surrounded them, the screams of the dying, the rage of those still living and fighting, some still bond had been forged between the two. The Arab extended his sword hand, having sheathed his weapon oblivious, it seemed, to the mayhem around them, and helped Robin to his feet, then turned away to mount his horse. Robin moved after him in astonishment and coming up to his stirrup grasped at the reins of his horse to stop him moving.

The Arab turned to him and Robin could only speak his question with his face, "Why did you not kill me?"

They gazed at each other for that timeless wordless moment which was filled with an eternity of knowledge and the Arab leant down and patted him on the breast saying only, "Muslim, Muslim," and then rode away from him into the fray, unsheathing his sword again, as he did, for fresh killing.

"Imam," Robin told me on his deathbed nary an hour before he fired that last tremendous arrow, "From that day nothing could ever be the same again. It was that day that put me in this forest here, an outlaw in my own land, I who never willingly broke a law of God nor man in my whole life," and he wept, though not I feel in sorrow but overwhelmed by some other powerful arousal of emotion in his bosom.

"Imam," he had continued, "Let my story be told. We are early comers, we are too early I fear. Others will come, later, much later. They must know, they must know."

And so I write. For Robin saw the churlish and

treacherous behaviour of him we knew to be the Cravenheart, the massacres of the helpless, the breaking of oaths, the rape of the women. You might blame some of that on the troops but it must be that the leader carries the terrible responsibility for his men. And what a contrast when that noble lord, Salahuddin Ayyubi, he they call Saladdin, set free most magnanimously his enemies and the captives when he took Jerusalem. If truth be told, why, his noble conduct won that war more than force of arms.

Yet none of that was sufficient to convert my troubled Squire Robin of Loxley from the religion of his ancestors. Rather, the meeting with the ancient and venerable Shaykh Burhanuddin was the matter that settled the affair. It fell in this manner. Robin sought high and low for some things that the Abbot had asked of him, including some manuscripts of long-lost gospels in the Syriac tongue or Aramaic. Long-lost I say but truly they had been destroyed by mother church along with the poor folk who had the temerity to possess copies and how many they had been! Rumour long had circulated in the West that certain churches of the eastern rite had secreted various fabulous texts, and seekers of truth such as the old Abbot thirsted after them mightily.

While engaged, during one of the frequent truces, in trying to find such a manuscript, which demanded much intercourse with Arabic-speaking Christians, who might often appear to have more in common with Mahometans than with Christian folk, Robin was wandering alone and unprotected through a little Arabic market place in some small town. He told me that he felt closer and closer to the goal of what the Abbot required of him and so he became excited as if the very spirit of the old man were running in his veins. Thus was he so incautious as to be totally alone in this dangerous land, surrounded by treacherous infidels. There it happened that he was greeted by two beardless youths who insisted on taking him by the hand and leading him somewhere. They were so evidently worthy beings and Robin always the most trusting of men, even sometimes when he ought for his own sake to have taken more care, that he followed them, they leading him like a little child wherever they willed.

Glory be to God, and did they not lead him to a simple little house in one of those twisty little back-streets that run through their beehives cities, their rabbit-warren towns? In the house sat an old man, the very age and mirror image of the venerable Abbot, yet I don't mean in physique but in his being. That old Shaykh, Shaykh Burhanuddin sat in front of a plate of food enough for two with two small loaves of the Arab bread before him, patiently waiting. The food was piping hot and he did not look at all surprised to see what the Arab youths had brought him. He merely motioned our Robin to sit down and then with great dignity he pronounced "*Bismillah*" which we since learnt means "In the name of Allah," and, signalling to Robin to commence, he began to eat.

"Imam, I tell you that neither of us said a word, for we had no word in common, yet by the end of that meal I was a Muslim," Robin told me.

"But how could that be, Robin?" I queried him.

"Scarce can I tell, yet I hazard that if you had sat there with that old man you could have done naught else," Robin said, scratching his head, searching for the words to tell me of it, for he was ever a man of action never really a man of words, "All I can say is that that man sat with God, ate with God, slept with God, talked with God, saw God, heard God and knew little but God. I never saw the like of him before or since but I knew that if this was a Mahometan then I was a Mahometan, I mean a Muslim."

When he told me the story, as he often did, Robin himself reflected some of the glow from that meeting, so that it was as if I could see that Shaykh sitting before me bathed in the presence of God, eating simple and humble food with a man he was supposed to be at war with.

"When I left he put a gold coin in my hand and kissed me on the forehead and I smelled the beautiful musk smell that came from him," Robin told and retold me in wonder, "He entrusted me to the two youths who appeared, as if out of nowhere, and took me to another man, Adnan. Adnan spoke some of my language and a bit of the Frankish lingo and he taught me the basics of being a Muslim. He taught me how to wash for the prayer and he led me in prayer five times a day for the days I was there.

"'We not go to mosque now. It not good for you. You, me, pray together here, house,' he said, 'Wine no good. Pig – bad meat. *Riba, riba, riba* …?' and I could see that he was searching for the right word in my language. Then we took a long time miming and acting out what it was for I could see that he saw it was very important for me to know. 'Usury!' I suddenly cried out. 'Yes, usury,' he answered, delighted that I had understood, 'Very bad. Worse – murder, worse – other man's wife, worse – killing, worse – stealing, worse – dead drunk. Very bad. God,' and he gestured heavenward, 'God hate. God make war. Usury – *riba* very bad. God make war. We make war,' and he stopped, exhausted by the effort of trying to convey his thought. He gave me much to think about, for, as you know Imam, the church is the fountainhead of all usury in our unhappy land."

"Another day he taught me about *jihad*. 'Call people to God,' he ordered me. There was a whole lot more about offering to let Christians and Jews live under Muslim governance for the payment of four gold coins, each adult male, every year.

"But from the moment I landed on English soil my hands were never empty of a weapon. It was a fight from the first moment. I had no chance even to summon them to Islam. When the story went around that I was a renegade all hands were against me.

"He had taught me the rules of raiding parties. 'You take all booty, all booty,' and I learnt that I was to gather the booty together, take a fifth of it myself and divide the rest among the men equally. I learnt that the Prophet Muhammad, may God bless him and grant him peace, had then given and given from his fifth of the booty until it was all gone.

"Imam, you have seen, we have raided and we have plundered these despoilers of our people and our land. You have seen my fifth go to the poor and the needy, and there are plenty of them in this accursed age. None of the fifth was left for me. You have seen my men divide up the other four-fifths fairly. Many of them have been most generous with their portions too. Tell the people our story," and here he had coughed and it had come up bloody. We had looked at each other and the knowledge of death was in his face.

"Imam, it will never be mentioned even that we were Muslims, they have covered it all over. Imam let them know," and with this he had coughed again.

I reached down and felt his toes, "Robin can you feel this?" I asked, giving them a pinch and he said, "No."

I reached up and felt his knees and also pinched them, "Can you feel this?" and he told me, "No."

"Then Robin Nuruddin of Loxley prepare to die, for it is very close," I remember telling him with tears running down my face, for I loved him as I have never loved any other man and was deeply hurt that the Lord was taking him and leaving me here alone.

He pulled himself up maybe an inch or so and raised the forefinger on his right hand and repeated in Arabic first and then in our English tongue, "I bear witness that there is no god, only Allah alone without partner. And I bear witness that Muhammad is His slave and messenger whom He sent as a mercy to all mankind and as a warner and bringer of good news and I bear witness that Jesus is

His slave and messenger and …," and then he slumped back sightless but with a light in his face, so that it was as if he was telling me again of that marvellous old Shaykh Burhanuddin. Thus passed Robin of Loxley, Nuruddin, he they call Robin Hood.

And I, Friar as I was, Imam as I am, Abdullah Tuck bear witness to what he bore witness and I also witness that Robin Hood was the best man of his age in England. You cannot understand him and what he fought for unless you know that he fought a just fight according to the way of Muhammad, may God bless him and grant him peace, taking from the wealthy Norman barons and church usurers, giving to the starving poor of the parishes. I have heard the ballads that are being sung about us now. They, none of them, have understood anything. People! Worship your Lord! Follow Muhammad, may God bless him and grant him peace! Take to prayer! Establish the poor tax on your wealth. Rise up against the moneylenders! Eat clean food! See that justice is done and not only the law! Above all see that justice is done!

DRACULA

They entered with some trepidation through the castle's creaking door and stood within the great hall, awed slightly by the sternly silent butler's presence.

"Is your master at home?" Egmont ventured, "I think that he is expecting us."

The butler glanced ever so imperceptibly at the window behind their heads through which could be seen the lurid sunset.

He said evenly, "I think sir, that he might be at home. If you will permit me I will go and enquire." His bearing had a touch of insolence masked only so slightly by his impeccable formality.

Egmont and Wallace looked at each other as the man withdrew up the vast winding staircase into the remotenesses of the castle.

"You can just imagine this great hall lit with flaming brands," Wallace remarked jovially, trying somehow to dispel the solemnity which hovered around the place and settled on their hearts, "You can see why the Dracula legend arose around these parts. Transylvania is not the most heartening of surroundings."

Egmont looked at him sharply, a look that tried to

penetrate to his inmost, but the remark, he saw, had not come from there but from the superficial froth of his consciousness. Wallace nevertheless was not slow to note the alertness that his thoughtless words had summoned up in the other man.

"Have you ever read Bram Stoker's work, Egmont?" he continued, the kind of question one asks when one is trying to while away some minutes, nervously perhaps.

"I have, of course," Egmont replied abruptly, "But one does not need to know the original in these cases, for the popular filmed versions reveal a great deal about the psyches of those who make them and those who watch them." He smiled conspiratorially towards Wallace, removing any sense of having put him in his place.

"Somehow the electricity has not changed the eerie quality of this place at all," Wallace ventured, "That is assuming that it had originally an eerieness, perhaps it is solely due to the electric lighting, the essential eerieness of technology." And his remarks had the feel of whistling in the dark while ambling through the graveyard, they only heightened the sense of unease.

"Don't underestimate the genuine evil and malice that lurk in this place," Egmont retorted, refusing to whistle away or ignore the ghosts of the place. Yet Egmont's presence was more reassuring to Wallace than his own wishful thinking was to himself.

"Very rude of them to leave us standing here," Egmont went on, "He's been away a long time really."

They fell silent contemplating the paintings on the

ascending stairwell, a long succession of rather grim and morbid looking fellows, and women who looked emaciated somehow from within.

"Cheerful lot!" Wallace thought.

"My master will see you now," the voice spoke from behind them and they wheeled round to face the butler who had addressed them from a door through which they could see a rather narrow passage and then stairs leading down into the depths.

"How did he go upstairs and then return from the basement?" Wallace quizzed himself, not even asking the question consciously but rather as a puzzled tickling in a corner of his thinking of which he was only dimly aware.

The man strode towards a rather large door which he threw creakily open revealing the library and then he stood back waiting for the two men to enter. The room they came into was lit with one of those blazing log fires that filled the huge hearth, the library shelves were lined with volume upon volume of dusty, leather bound books. The chairs and sofa too were old red-leather and the floor was carpeted by an ageing dark red Persian carpet which in another context might have been cheerful but in this somehow added only to the genuine darkness that no electric lights could dispel.

Egmont took off his coat and handed it to the butler whose impassive face refused to reveal the assumption of authority by the other man and how distasteful it was to him.

As if to rub in what he had done Egmont by an almost

imperceptible nod to Wallace urged him to give his coat also to the man-servant, "And oh by the way, our bags are still in the car, perhaps you could arrange to have them brought in," and Egmont stood face-to-face with the man and it was as if the shadows in the room leapt back several metres. The butler retired from the room with that obsequiousness which masks the arrogance of a servant who has become indispensable to his master and thus master of him. He was deeply angered to have been put in his place by this rather unlikely middle-aged man.

Wallace threw himself in a chair, trying in his own way to take the signal from the other man's assertion of authority and lordship of the situation. Radical steps needed to be taken to dispel the gloom that hung like a pall of smoke over the meeting.

"Good evening Professor Egmont, Mr Wallace," and the two men looked around startled to see a previously undiscovered door in a recess between two library shelves. There stood a rather tall and distinguished looking gentleman, who was almost indecently handsome in what Egmont was later to describe as 'the Dorian Gray mode'. Tall with aquiline features, black hair with just a blaze of silver, enough to lend him that sense of belonging to the aristocracy. When others went grey-haired, the aristocracy silvered.

"Good evening, Count," Egmont responded.

"How kind of you to come all this way to see me," the Count spoke graciously as he elegantly almost glided across the room to shake hands with them. Indeed

Wallace found it difficult to believe that he used the ordinary form of locomotion at all, so effortlessly did he seem almost to hover and skate over the floor. They all returned to sit on the leather suite.

"How could I refuse such a generous invitation," Egmont countered.

"Professor I have admired your work for years," the Count spoke, "And of all the people working in the arena of our Transylvanian heritage your work is really the most original."

"I too could not have passed up the opportunity of meeting someone I have known about for so long," Egmont.

"You flatter me Professor," the Count looked almost startled, "I am afraid that I am rather a non-entity in Transylvania, relic of a past order which will never return."

"You do yourself an injustice, Count," Egmont urbanely countered, "For your reputation will long outlive mine," and he looked at the other with his penetrating gaze but the Count merely stood and turned away to walk towards the fireplace. There he warmed himself. Wallace had the distinct impression that he was thrown off-balance by his friend's demeanour.

"Professor, I have long been fascinated by your views on our deplorable Count Vlad and his linkage to the origins of the Dracula myth," the Count instigated his opening gambit, perhaps a little early Wallace thought and maybe because Egmont threw him so out of key, so wrong-footed him.

There was a slight pause and then the Count somehow found himself, "But forgive me, you have come such a long way and it is most discourteous of me to launch so quickly into the purpose of our meeting. You must wash from the journey, dress and we will have dinner at seven, yes seven," and he looked thoughtfully towards the door. The two men following his gaze had just time to see the domineering butler glide off down the corridor.

Quite directly a maid servant appeared, but yet again she had a rather cold and arrogant air about her, not that of one given to serve, but of one given to rule.

"Perhaps this is just the manner of these Transylvanians," Wallace mused, "Rum lot altogether."

The men were shown to their rooms and Wallace found himself wishing that they were not split up but allowed to share a bedroom. In other circumstances he would have appreciated his own private rooms but he was on the point of asking to be permitted to share with Egmont when he caught the other's knowing look and warning glance and withheld his words. He was not much put at his ease by the room either, with yet more of the ancestral portraits glowering down on him, as if they encapsulated the essential malignant spirit of the dead ancestor, some determination to outlive the grave even if it should be at tremendous cost. Wallace was greatly relieved to descend for dinner at its hour although it meant more of the Count's sombre company.

It was over the after-dinner wine that the conversation

began to move away from the channels of rather stilted small talk which the Count had contrived to lead the discussion through. Or rather it would have been over the wine if Egmont had not refused it and asked for a cup of coffee instead.

The Count had raised his eyebrows, "You don't drink, Professor?" he queried, "Quite unusual in our age, is it not?"

"Less and less unusual, Count," Egmont replied, strenuously avoiding Evan's gaze, for Wallace was shocked to find Egmont, whom he knew to appreciate a glass of wine, pretending to be a teetotaller.

"A recent decision, Professor, perhaps or is it part of a longer term abstinence?" the Count asked.

"An extremely recent decision, Count," Egmont replied, "Oh don't get me wrong, I'm no killjoy, but I've come to know of other ... intoxicants ..." and he glanced at the Count, "... for which the consumption of wine is a definite contra-indication."

Wallace, for no reason that he could give himself, when asked by the Count, "And you Mr Wallace?" admitted to being also tee-total, although not half an hour before meeting the Count he had sipped some best Scotch from his travelling flask. His instinct told him that here, total preservation of the intellect might be of paramount importance.

And so the conversation drifted and limped from academic trivialities to intellectual banalities, tediously well past midnight and on into the wee small hours and the hour known as the hour of the wolf.

"Count Dracula, of course his origin was in the horrific career of Vlad the Impaler," Egmont seized the initiative and launched into his topic, the one which had occupied him, at some times almost to the detriment of his academic career, increasingly over the past years, "And of course there are many views of the secret of the power of the legend. It undoubtedly touches on something in the psyche."

Wallace glanced towards his host and was shocked to find a definite unhinged look about his features, tinged with a certain malevolence, which only heightened the familial resemblance with his abhorrent ancestors.

"I'm sorry Count to mention it, but you look quite upset by what Professor Egmont just said, as if somehow it was an attack on you personally," Wallace, with almost a degree of malice, could not resist interjecting. Somehow he was pleased to see the overbearing old aristocrat cornered like a badger.

The Count turned his gaze, now regained its sardonic and haughty remoteness towards Wallace, who had the distinct impression that he was a small grub that some rather austere biologist was considering dissecting for the sheer pleasure of seeing it squirm.

"Mr Wallace, I am sure you are aware that Count Vlad was one of my ancestors," he spoke with the condescension of an elderly schoolmaster reprimanding a gauche teenager for misconjugating a Latin verb, "And it is by no means the consensus here in Transylvania and particularly not in my family that his career was . . . horrific." The lamps seemed to quail before the darkness which pressed in upon the little dinner party.

The butler came in and with his awful pretence at obsequiousness, whispered something in his master's ear and then withdrew.

"But horrific, nonetheless, it was, Count," Egmont pressed on, "A wholesale butchery of Muslims by having them dropped on spikes, and all in the name of Christianity the religion of love and peace! What could be more awful than that, that and all the other atrocities committed in the name of love by so-called Christians."

The Count blanched and recovering his composure smiled, "I think you are almost unique, Professor in having brought out the religious dimensions of the myth, rather than the psycho-sexual, as have done the Freudians among others."

"The Freudians did indeed pick on the phallic symbolism of the stakes the Impaler used, the rather bizarre concept of his having converted his victims into excrement and a lot of stuff which I have come to suspect tells one more about the workings of a Freudian's mind than anything else. They shed little light here. But now my dear Count, I have also come to understand those very psycho-sexual impulses so clearly contained in the . . . myth," and Egmont lingered over the last word with a sense of irony which puzzled Wallace, who thought that he knew Egmont's work in this area inside out.

The Count blanched again but regaining his composure

tried very hard to maintain a kind of academic detachment to his side of the contest which was so clearly a struggle of wills, a test of two male beings locked in combat, yet with all of the niceties of civilised and polite society.

"I use the word myth advisedly since we are also dealing with a historical Vlad as well as the psycho-sexual myth which was grown larger than him to such an extent that most have never heard of Vlad the Impaler," Egmont resumed, "Yet I suggest that both the history and the Hollywood tale are vital and that they synergistically feed each other."

Wallace thought that his friend was being rather pompous.

The Count was attempting to maintain his rather forced look of admiring interest in Egmont's discourse, although the almost malevolent intent in his cold eyes could have escaped no-one.

"Let us put the case as best we can," Egmont leant forward energetically on his chair and grasped the hot coffee cup and vigorously raised it to his lips. The strong black drink was sugarless but had turned into a whitish-brown with a generous dose of the Transylvanian cream. He sipped at it pensively, aware that he held the floor and that the Count was almost helpless before him.

"Dracula, let us be frank, is the repressed Christian erotic drive," Egmont launched into the argument, "He is repressed rather than sublimated and so he emerges as an evil force. He has to come out somewhere. He comes out at night and preys on beautiful innocent virgin women."

"I must take you to task Professor for your particularising the repressed erotic drive as Christian. None of the Freudians saw the need to label it as anything but a repressed drive," the Count entered the combat, "For repression is repression whether the owner is a Christian, Muslim or Jew."

"Touché. But Dracula is very much a Christian historically," Egmont countered, "And by no accident, for repression is entirely a Judaeo-Christian phenomena."

Wallace was becoming bored by what he saw as armchair academics' tall-talk.

"You see, certain recent developments have forced me to take a very radically different view even from that I previously held," Egmont went on, "I have come to an understanding. The man Jesus, peace be upon him, was one of the Children of Israel, following the law of Moses, except that he never married."

"Of course," the Count murmured, although there had been a flicker of response to that 'the man Jesus' which he had held in check upon hearing the blessings of peace, his eyebrows rising ever so slightly with an unspoken question and a dawning realisation.

"He had never married. The so-called Christians, who should really have been Jews, and the early ones of whom really were Mosaic Jews, inventing a pseudo-religion and dating everything from a new year zero, were forced to consider celibacy the norm and monogamy a concession to human nature's frailty. Polygamy of course was totally outside the pale, so to speak," Egmont pressed home his point, "The situation for the whole of history outside of this bizarre two millennia in this parochial corner of the planet has been that polygamy is the natural form of man, monogamy a concession and celibacy an in-between condition for those temporarily unable to marry or consumed for a period with travelling the spiritual path. But celibacy was never a permanent state in itself!"

"I do not really see what the connection is to Dracula, Professor," and hear Wallace felt forced to burst in from his genuine boredom at the line the whole thing was taking.

"Quite simple Wallace," and here it was the Count who spoke, "The Professor sees Dracula as a prototypical Christian, if I am not mistaken, bound, in theory at least, to celibacy as a norm thus experiencing his erotic drive as a threatening malignant force. Thus far and only so far do I understand," and the Count turned towards the Professor.

The butler hastened into the room with a slightly flustered and alarmed look on his face carrying in his right hand a rather old-fashioned fob-watch connected by a leather strap to one of his pockets. He bent solicitously over the Count and they had a minor confabulation both glancing nervously towards the eastern windows and back and forward to the watch. The Count imperiously dismissed his arrogant underling who retreated from the scene looking considerably alarmed.

"Please continue Professor," the Count said.

"The Muslim is polygamous and thus for Vlad he represents everything that he has repressed, for even if he has a thousand virgins delivered to his castle, it is never in the broad light of day but a pandering to his repressed and dark nature," the Professor spoke with animation, "Thus he impales that which he loves, the Muslim, his own authentic and natural being. Dracula preys on beautiful innocent and virgin women, draining them of their life, turning them into mini-versions of himself. He cannot bond with them so must live parasitically off them, transmuting them by his contact from the pure virgin beauty of women into horrors. In one way he is Don Juan, Don Giovanni and in another way he is King Midas."

The Count's complexion was the most alarming greyish white, but more disturbing were the reds around his eyes and the periodic elements of green to be seen in his pale grey skin, "Most intriguing indeed Professor."

"There is more," and now the Professor was relentless, seeing the clear effect he was having on his distinguished opponent's academic detachment, "He becomes the very embodiment of the repressed erotic drive for Christendom itself. Look at the legend. Dracula only comes out at night. He lives off the beautiful and unsuspecting. He pollutes whatever he touches. He can be countered by the Cross, the only symbol he fears, the symbol of Christian celibacy and suffering, the suffering of repressed naturalness, it forces him to retreat back into his coffin to rest the day and return again another night."

"Count! Count!" and here the butler entered most un-butlerly remonstrating openly with his master, gesticulating towards the open east windows where the beginnings of a dim dawn light were just to be seen, the watch in his hand, arguing in a thick and incomprehensible Transylvanian tongue.

The Count appeared to acquiesce with his servant and rose as if to leave, "My butler is over concerned for my welfare, Professor, as you see. Please excuse me. My lifestyle and my age require of me particular attention to diet and the regimen of sleep. I must have some nourishment and rest and perhaps we can resume this most enlightening discussion at another point, if you would deign to rest here as my guests for another day," and he looked distractedly from Egmont to Wallace, who for courtesy's sake he included in his old-world glance.

"I'm afraid that won't be possible, Count," Professor Egmont said quite loudly, "Our work here is over and we must be on our ways. Indeed I too would like to continue our conversation further to its conclusion but there are certain distractions which mean I should interrupt it at this moment for some minutes. Perhaps we might resume our interrupted discussion for just a few minutes when you have had your nourishment? I promise you it should not delay you from your much needed rest."

Wallace looked with total bafflement at the two men, realising that some game was in progress between two giants of which he had only the dimmest inklings as to its nature. He saw vaguely that some challenge was presented to the Count who felt it hard to refuse.

"Certainly Professor, how could I miss such an

opportunity?" and both men retired from the room, leaving Wallace to contemplate the dawn creeping over the horizon in a rather sluggish fashion. He glanced around the library for the first time, in incomprehension at the Transylvanian titles that lined the bookshelves, and then in surprise at the rather large number of evidently Christian volumes in Latin and other tongues which he could pick out. The Count surprised him, for his rather urbane exterior seemed to preclude any specific religious commitment. He was still standing in puzzlement gazing at some of those titles when the Count's voice behind him startled him, "Yes, I am a Christian of sorts, Mr Wallace."

"Rather rare in Christendom these days, Count?" Wallace tried to say in a forced jocularity, glancing at the Count's rather healthier complexion, which yet gave him no ease, for his pallor seemed the basic condition and it was only slightly alleviated by the red of life-giving blood.

"Not at all Wallace. In fact rather more common that you perhaps realise," the voice of the Professor interrupted both their reveries. Wallace looked towards him and saw him refreshed and renewed in some other manner than from the taking of nourishment, yet he saw him more genuinely nourished and refreshed. These things puzzled him greatly as he sat down for the last part of their discussion. The Count remained standing as if to underline the fact that the rest of the conversation was to have a rather limited time allotted to it. The Professor moved to the bookcase.

"Christendom may even have few who consciously feel

Christian, Wallace but it is unmistakably Christendom nonetheless," and Egmont lingered over the titles, "Yet as we have seen that seems to have become disconnected from Christ, somehow. It is something else. There is an element in the myth, the other element which results in the destruction of Dracula, although he does appear to come back repeatedly in film after film. It is that direct sunlight destroys him. I suspect that if there were a real Dracula alive today that would not prove literally true, that if one were at the mercy of this bestial demonic force one would not be saved by the rising of the sun," and he looked towards the Count whose face betrayed a certain sardonic amusement, indeed, as Egmont talked he had with some nonchalance resumed his seat.

"What does the destruction from light represent then, if it is purely myth, Professor," Wallace asked, more because he felt that his trusted friend was in need of the question in order to continue his line of thought, than from his own desire to ask.

"Much have I pondered this," Egmont said, his eyes taking on an inward cast, as if he were looking deep into his being to find the right thoughts, and as if they were of paramount importance at this juncture of his life, "Light symbolises truth, goodness and the Divine. These are almost universal. So it is the truth, goodness and the light of the Divine which banish Dracula forever."

"Your argument has one flaw," the Count broke in.

"I know it, indeed, Count," Egmont broke out, "But I need to hear *you* say it."

"Dracula, as you so brilliantly have proved in your numerous works, is already a Christian," and the Count spoke with a degree of superiority and superciliousness which Wallace found most provocative, "Therefore he is on the side of the true, the good and the Divine, in his own way."

"Not true!" Egmont shouted almost with triumph, "But I am so pleased that you should advance the thought."

The Count had a haughty distance to his demeanour and an imperious remoteness, as if far above the childish manoeuvres of his brilliant opponent, yet Wallace was sure that he detected a tremor of anxiety run across his features.

"But he is a perfect metaphor for the Christian dilemma, indeed," Egmont continued, intrigued by his own line of thought, "I must admit that it is only very recently that all the pieces of the puzzle have fallen into place for me, otherwise I was loath to accept your invitation. Imagine Dracula if you will and his atrocious dilemma. You must also take into account those impaled Muslims of his, they are the key which I needed for the final decoding. He could have remained mortifying the flesh, a misogynistic hermit with the occasional lapse, but then he is Christian, he is guaranteed salvation so none of that matters, the mere fact of his believing guarantee him salvation, no matter what degradation he sinks to. This must be understood to know the true horror of Dracula."

Wallace had never seen his friend speak with the passion and conviction that he now did. He glanced towards the Count and was taken aback to see him tremble with genuine agitation. Egmont was so taken up in the workings of his thought that he did not look at him and did not see the dismay that was travelling across his pallid face.

"It was those Muslims, happily polygamous, men and women, quite content," Egmont went on, "Oh, of course, one should never idealise anything and life is contradictions, conflict, divorce is as much a part of the whole picture, jealousy, strife, husband and wife. Our Christian cannot accept the humanness of it all, he is bound to become other than human, to suffer and be transfigured, utterly non-human. He must turn the other cheek, he must take up his cross, and so-what if he also puts the other on a cross, it is all a necessary part of this whole ghastly picture of suffering towards the divine-human."

The two listeners were transfixed to their seats, the dawn bleakly outlining them from behind, the light of the sun bloodying the sky in a most ominous crimson as if to underline the horrid bloody poetry of the Christianity so gorily painted.

"Before Islam, Vlad might have been just an unhappy sinner, a tortured Christian ascetic with his lapses, but there they are before him happy in carnality, seeing no split in existence between their prayer and their intercourse," Egmont held them and himself in thrall to the power of his idea, "And they invite him to it! Oh his terrible indecision, his being drawn to it. And who are they? Are they in fact Transylvanian Bogomils, Cathars and Albigensians, the poor remnants of the authentic teaching of the man Jesus, who held out for centuries despite the persecution, the bloody torture of the official church, the fiendish torture machine that is the Church? And what do they hold out for? Why, the one who is to come, who has been foretold, the bringer of God's Kingdom on Earth. In the Prophet of Islam, Muhammad, may Allah bless him and grant him peace, they joyfully recognise him, even after the centuries, and become Muslims. The Transylvanian Muslims were Transylvanians, kith and kin. Vlad is drawn to their joy, but held by his masochistic addiction to suffering and as we all know masochism too easily turns into sadism, and Vlad the Impaler is born. Perhaps, he has some higher reasoning, he tortures them for their own good, hoping that while they die writhing in agony, screaming their confessions, they will agree to worship any god if he will just kill them and let them go. But they don't. That is the final shock. They simply do not. Excuse me, I cannot go on."

It was as if a spell had been broken and the three men suddenly returned to the twenty-first century in their little Transylvanian castle. They blinked at each other in the rapidly mounting light of dawn.

Egmont was yet the first man to rouse from the trance his talk had left them in, "I have to admit gentlemen that I had to make a couple of radical decisions before I came here, for my own good and safety. One, I accepted Islam," and the two men sat back suddenly as if they had been struck in the face. Wallace was perhaps if anything the more shocked of the two, the Count reacting more as if he had received a blow that he had long been anticipating.

"You changed religion?" Wallace charged, "But in this scientific and secular age that is just a step sideways, it makes no sense."

"It only makes sense when you see that this scientific and secular age as you call it, is indeed the direct extension of the Christian nightmare of witch-burning, or rather women-burning. It is only cosmetically different," Egmont replied, "It only made any sense to me when I looked at it in the light of number. It seemed on a cursory glance to be the One against the Three-in-one. When I understood that our age is really the age of the Two which are never One, then I had to move."

The Count's face was dangerously red and Wallace registered his expression with some alarm, seeing the glimmering threat of malignancy poised to strike.

"Count what do you make of it all?" Wallace blurted, "As a committed Christian you must have some views on it?"

"Trinity is an essential element of the Christian faith. Which One of the Three are you going to remove to arrive at your Two, Professor?" the Count with the last ounce apparently of his self-control, spoke his question almost in a whisper, the sound of which chilled Wallace to the bone. Egmont appeared not to notice the threat of evil in it and looking into the distance continued with his theme, or rather would have if the butler had not entered yet again and thrown the most fantastic Transylvanian fit of exasperation, motioning almost pathetically to the looming light of the imminent rising sun. The Count, in a voice full of menace, said a few phrases and the man, like a balloon punctured, slunk from the room. "Please continue, Professor Egmont, we shall not be interrupted again."

"A true dualism is composed of light and dark, good and evil, whereas the trinity is a trinity of good, a theologian's apple pie, which nobody has ever really understood, especially not the theologians. It is the very essence of the control structure that was the torturing christian church that it should demand confession of a patent absurdity. Imagine the sadistic delight of the tyrant at having extorted from his subject population a confession of such an obvious piece of gobbledygook, why, there can be no more complete proof of total state power than that! It is the power of the bully, 'I am telling you that the moon is made of green cheese, anyone who disagrees with me is for it,' and so they agree because he has the force, 'OK, if you say so, the moon is made of green cheese.'"

"You haven't told us really of your Two, Professor," the Count almost hissed, sending quivers of fear up and down Wallace' spine.

"Count, it was only when I understood that there is only One, that I understood the Two," Egmont far from being alarmed, almost chortled, "Reality is only One, there is only One force in existence, the Divine Who has total power, all knowledge and is All-merciful."

"And the dark force?" Wallace queried, possibly alarmed that his addiction to horror movies was to be undermined.

"There is none. The One is truly One and has no opposite. Yet in the world we inhabit, the seeming world of all the things, all the beings, one particular being refuses, the one called Satan, the Devil and Shaytan in Arabic," Egmont paused briefly, "But he is only a creature and he has a function within the plan, he must test Man who is the purpose and meaning of the whole. Satan has no power except what man gives him, he only has force and power if man allows him to have it, allows him to direct his life. Yet poor Christianity is caught in this bogie-man world of God and the Devil, and it carries on throughout our culture, the cult of the dark; from the devil, to Star Wars, the war of the Black and the White. Reality, though is not black and white, it is multi-coloured, a beautiful spectrum of colourful shadings."

"So the destruction of Dracula by the light?" Wallace interjected.

"The light of reality is that he never existed, unless you give him existence; that is the light which destroys him, he is truly a myth," Egmont said quietly and with dignity, "He is the devil, who is a nobody, a slime, a slinking whisperer. Don't underestimate him though, but he is not a black evil godly power. Dracula is a myth, the decoding of which shows you the workings of Christian dualism, he is a manifestation of Christian devil worship. Yes! for by ascribing power to the devil they made him a god."

And as they talked the sun rose above the horizon and shone full upon them, blood-red but no longer with threat and menace. The Count blinked bleerily, looking now exactly the rather old and frail man that he really was, and Wallace could see that he was very tired by their night's intellectual exertions and genuinely needed to rest. The Count pulled on the bell-rope which hung to hand and Boris, the old butler advanced from the shadows which concealed yet another surprise doorway ready to help the aged Count to his bed.

BILLY THE KID

He rose slightly in the saddle. Shading his steely grey eyes from the blazing desert sun, he gazed long and intently at the remote and barren horizon. Billy looked for the tell-tale signs of the posse. He looked for that ominous dust-cloud that bespoke a body of mounted men. The Indians left no such trails across the sky. They could be right upon you before you knew it. Yet Billy had established a certain unspoken rapport with the Indian. They and he had their backs to the wall. The enemy was the same in both cases – greed and avarice. Although nothing had been said, they recognised him and he them.

The horizon told no tale. Billy sought the nearest shade to hide out the rest of that mercilessly hot day. The posse's horizon would tell no tale either.

Thus had it gone for some time now. Billy had once been, of all young men, the most law-abiding. He was now a fugitive from the most servile murderous scum he had ever seen. They were servile to money, servile to the highest bidder, servile to the devil. He was a fugitive because they had sheriffs' stars pinned to their breasts. Being law-abiding had never been enough for Billy. He had had to go around reforming, putting wrongs to right. He could never shut up in the face of an injustice, especially one done to an underdog.

"Goddamnit Pa, it's clear!" he'd shouted at his father, "It's against the word of your God!" Of course there had been enough men willing to nod their heads sagely and sympathetically. But when the bankers came for the Reynolds' ranch Billy was the only one there to say to them, "No!"

"Shucks Billy, I got no quarrel with you. This is the Reynolds farm," O'Callaghan had said, "Mr Reynolds, it's the guys back east. They told us we got to come up with some bucks pronto or they'll close our branch down. I ain't got no quarrel with neither of you and if you'll just . . ."

"Jimmy O'Callaghan, you're the man who's come with your crew to take Mr Reynold's farm," Billy drawled, "I don't see no eastern fellas here. If you don't get off Mr Reynold's land fast, it's you I'll shoot. There has to be someone I can shoot and I sure can't afford the fare to Philadelphia."

Then of course someone had pulled a gun. There was a lot of shooting. They must have forgotten that not only was Billy the best shot for two hundred miles but the wildest ace in anyone's deck of cards.

And so he travelled now at night, a lone fugitive, to escape the eastern bankers' posse. They were never 'lawmen'. He thought of all the events that drove him down his lonely trail. He felt very good indeed. And all that he wished for were other men who would be men enough to live beside him, fight the banks beside him and die beside him, fighting like men against the wrong and the mediocre. But the young men whom he had grown up with, sons of ranchers, were all training to be bank clerks! So he'd fight them too.

And Billy wished, ached and longed for a woman, who'd be there to welcome him home. Someone to support him in his fight but not hold him back when he had to go out, perhaps to die. Someone who'd see that he got a decent burial, who'd maybe cry and miss him. But someone who would have a dead hero for a husband rather than a spineless skunk, a slimeball who'd work for the bank which was taking the land, pushing railroads across the majestic wilderness and having all the buffalo shot.

"Your granddaddies came to this land to build the Kingdom of God on earth!" he had lectured the townsfolk from on top of his soap-box outside the bank. The terrified clerks ran here and there to find a sheriff or a deputy man enough or fool enough to face Billy the Kid. "And you folks know the Bible. You know usury is forbidden. You know Jesus threw them out of the Temple. You can't let them take over America. They're actually doing it in front of your eyes."

"Aw Billy, what can we do? They buy the sheriffs. They buy the mayors. They buy the judges. They own all the congressmen and the senators," called one rancher from the back. It was a motley assortment of people who'd gathered to hear this wild young blade harangue them.

"Your granddaddies came from the Old World to live

and be free here. They fought anyone who tried to stop them. They fought England and its King. They wanted to be free from the control of the Bank of England. I say we fight any bank, whether it's called the Bank of America or not, 'cause they'll take everything here like they have done in the Old World."

Musing later, Billy realised, without despair, that he was a man before his time. "Perhaps," he thought, "It has to get really bad before men will say, 'Hell, it's better to die honourable deaths than live like animals or slaves or worse.' Perhaps there will come a time when a bunch of men will stand together, shoulder to shoulder, and fight this thing that turns grown men into cissies."

And his soul revolted against the thought that he should be so absolutely alone. For a man must have a brother to stand by him. So it was that he thought of Pat Garret. And he resolved that after his daytime rest he'd set off to find him. Even as he decided that, he was uneasily aware that something in Pat made him unsettled. Pat was a man with some important choices he had yet to make. Yet Billy, having no friends at all and no choices before him, had nothing to lose.

"Pat," he said meditatively and then he paused. He carelessly took his gun and holster off for the first time in weeks. Billy was aware of the risk. But he knew that a man must have at least one person he can take his gun off with. "Pat, I need your help. I can't fight them alone."

"Billy, damnit!" Pat almost snarled, sobbed and wept

in the same breath, "You're an unsheathed blade. Every sword is out of its scabbard seeking your innards. Billy, there's ways and ways of fighting . . ."

"Like the way those smart city lawyers fight? They kill whole families with their smart pens. Should we fight like that?" and Billy spat in disgust. Then, calming himself by rolling a cigarette from Pat's aromatic tobacco and sprawling back in the high-backed chair, he resumed his drawl, "I scorn and despise those scum who so-casually sign away homes, lives and lands. I stand with the Indian and perhaps I'll fall with him. Everything we've got is tainted with the work of these book-keepers and cashiers. I'd prefer virtuous victory. But perhaps there is only honourable death left."

All the time Billy gazed into the log fire crackling. He was seemingly unaware of the wild alternations in Garret's facial expression. It veered between love, hate, despair, anguish, fear and indecision. That face was changing just as the log-fire cast its ever changing shadows over his visage.

"I've seen a lot of strange things, Pat," Billy continued his monologue, "The men I've fought and killed were fighting against the man in themselves. They wanted the man, the manliness within them, to lie down and die in front of the bank clerk in themselves. When they tried to kill me, they really tried to kill the man in themselves. Of course they died in the fight. They died, really, by their own hands."

"Good grief, Billy! You're talking like you've got a

mission from God, and all the angels guarding you!" and Pat would have burst into a loud guffaw but that Billy's direct cool gaze cut him short. A part of Pat's fear and hatred was his very real suspicion that Billy was a mad-dog killer and that he was to be the next victim.

"That I believe, Pat. I believe that if a man is a man he has a mission from God and angels guarding him. Any man at all," and he looked long and searchingly into his friend's anguished face, "And it frightens me and it frightens them and that's why they choose the devil, I guess. The devil is the easy option. The devil is the slippers by the fire."

"And you haven't, have you, oh no, you haven't chosen the devil, not Billy the Kid with seven men dead to his credit?" Pat spat out his words in anger and fever. It was a vain attempt to discharge a fraction of what bothered his soul, "You alone have chosen God and the angels. That gives you the right to kill whoever stands in front of you. Then you can say, 'Oh they killed themselves when they tried to fight me.' "

"Pat, I long for men to stand with me. I need brothers. There is no gunslinger whom I didn't plead with to stand shoulder-to-shoulder with me until we saw that justice was done," and Billy sat forward. Suddenly he was all animation. He looked intently into Pat's face, and said, "Join me. Pat, fight with me. Don't fight against me. I know they offered you money. I know they offered you a lot, but it's not worth it."

Even in the dim fire-light, the withdrawal of blood from Pat's face was clear as he blanched pale white.

"Pat, they can afford to offer you anything you like because they make money just by printing it – it's worth nothing more than a few cents – look!" and Billy took out a wad of dollar bills. He paused and then threw them on the fire. He laughed as Pat started in anxiety, "Pat, Pat, they're taking people's gold and silver away from them forever with these bits of paper. One day we'll all go in with a pile of it and say, 'I'd like my gold and silver back,' and they'll say, 'Sorry, can't do it. Orders from back east.' "

"Billy, you're too dangerous. There's no way they'll leave you alive," Pat almost sobbed.

"And don't I know it, Pat?" Billy said almost sombrely, "Yep, it's time for Billy the Kid to die. I came to you, Pat. I reckon you're the man to help me in that," and Billy sat back in his tall armchair and looked searchingly for a moment in Pat's eyes. He gazed again at the fire, no longer looking into his friend's baffled face.

"Billy, they offered me money, lots. I even got a down payment," and Pat excitedly and agitatedly reached inside his shirt for his leather wallet. It came out full of paper money. He threw it disgustedly in the fire, where it blazed besides Billy's wad.

The two men looked at each other.

"Pat, one man's a bandit, but two are a war party. That's what my Indian friends say," and they shook hands with great seriousness.

"Billy, if we go to, let's go out, guns blazing. I don't see any way that we can win. Let's take as many as we can with us, before they get us," Pat said eagerly.

"Why Pat, I'm shocked at you," Billy said, with mock seriousness, "I'd like to live a little bit longer, find me a woman, bring up some children. I don't really feel too much like just giving them my life on a plate. They certainly have enough gun-fighters and they don't really mind to lose a few. But I've only got the one me."

"Billy, I never thought to hear you say the coward's words," Pat said, reflectively.

"Pat, Pat! Just think," Billy said impassionedly, "We were two separate men and how weak and alone we were. Now we are two together and how strong we are already. Imagine if we were three, four, five…! Pat think if we were five hundred or a thousand. We have man's work. We have to find men to do it. Even if they are in China or Arabia, men and women. Pat, my old grandpappy was a doctor and he said to me that he used to think that when he cured somebody of a disease he had made them well. Then he realised that they were cured but they might not be well. He said that that's another thing, being well."

"Billy, I don't follow you at all," Pat drawled.

"If we fought them all and won, we wouldn't necessarily have a good society, Pat, that's what I mean," and Billy sat back, "We have more serious and demanding work, Pat, than taking out those bastards, which would be hard enough."

Pat sat up in his chair, both challenged and frightened.

"That is why Billy the Kid must die, killed, shot in the back by his old friend Pat Garret who'll pick up his reward. But this time not in paper but in gold, of course."

The two men turned, awed and slightly amazed, to the task in front of them.

OTELLO AND DESDEMONA

"Desdemona, only one thing mars this perfect happiness, this almost unbearable ecstasy I feel in our love for each other," spoke Otello, that tragic Moor, his head resting black on the snowy white bosom of beautiful Desdemona.

She looked at him with a face full of concern and sympathy, "Tell me beloved Otello, what it is that so troubles this moment of most serene peace," and it was as if she hoped to lift the burden of his distress by her willing attentiveness to his hidden fears.

"Dearest, you know something of my tale, my capture by the Saracens, my life of slavery, my subsequent escape and all my adventures, my heroic adventures," and he gave the word 'heroic' a curious and ironic twist, which dug into her heart, as if he had slighted the very element in him that she admired and loved most and so had insulted her. This thought she pushed away from her as he continued, "And as I hear my own adventures told and retold by you and by others, they are growing almost unrecognisable to me, as if they had happened to someone else. And we are at war with the

Saracen but I would extend to him the justice and fair treatment I know that he would afford me," and with these last words spoken most emphatically he snapped out of his reverie.

Desdemona sat up suddenly, forcing Otello also to rise. She drew her night-dress close around her bosom, as if to ward off a sudden chill that had invaded the warmth of her bedroom. "But they are heathens, savages, lost and doomed people …?" She was clearly unsettled by the line his talk was taking and so involuntarily crossed herself as she did in times of trouble, times when thoughts occurred or were presented to her which her intellect could not grasp.

"We know who the Saracen is. But I also know that the story is nowhere near as simple as our priests and troubadours would have us believe," and suddenly they had both shrunk from each other, so that they were now as far apart as they had previously been close together.

"What does he want with this probing?" she asked herself bitterly, "Why is it not enough to lie here with me, to share the wine of our love for each other?" and she came close to hating him as much as she had loved him.

"In truth, Desdemona dearest, my own people were a faithless and treacherous people, who lived a low and mean life, haunted by a thousand demons, my poor heathen African family," and he paused with infinite sadness on his face, which she could in no way understand, for if anything, she felt slightly repulsed by his African roots. She tried rather not to think about it and imagine him always as having come from some wonderful and exotic royal family, or from merchants perhaps in faraway and exciting places. Never did she try to see him squatting as a little naked brown baby on the sandy soil in some hut of straw and even cow-dung!

"I remember that raid so well," and Otello spoke now having regained his reverie with a far-away look in his eyes, "That raid when my mother and I were carried off into slavery."

She warmed to him again, for it was her admiration for his courage and bravery in adversity, his indomitable will to escape from the heathen which had won her heart to him, and along with that her pity for the privations and misery of slavery to such a wretched and pitiless foe as she felt the Saracen to be.

"But if I am just, my master was not a bad man," Otello admitted. Indeed he looked slightly hang-dog and guilty, perhaps a little sheepish at this admission, for had he not exploited the distaste with which the Saracen was held, extracting every ounce of advantage from it. "And why not?" he thought defensively, "I had been alone in all the world, far from my native land in more ways than one," of course he had pandered to his audience's prejudices.

Yet Desdemona, all unknown to Otello, was irritated beyond measure now, at the direction his discourse was taking, "Why are you dredging all of this unnecessary stuff up just precisely at the most perfect moment of peace we have ever known?" she asked him, only barely biting back on her resentment and hostility.

"Dearest, don't hold it against me but I have an awful

presentiment precisely at this very moment," and his anguished face stirred again the pity in her heart, "And it may be that what I have done is the cause of what is to happen, ah accursed presentiment, may it not prove true," and he buried his tortured face in her lap. Shocked, she ruffled his curly hair gently and consolingly.

"I don't know at all," and he looked beseechingly into her face, so that her constricted face melted and she forgave him yet again.

"Tell me dearest," she said, as encouragingly as she could muster.

"He sought of me to become a Muslim," he blurted, with a haunted and grey look about his noble black face, only to recover himself, "But I go too quickly perhaps."

She had to interrupt, for she could not understand this deep self-questioning that seemed to plague him, "Of course, we know that they tried to coerce you into their heathenish ways …"

But he broke in with impatience, "No! I must tell this story as it happened, not as it grew to suit its audience, not as I embellished and embroidered it for them," and he gestured to an imaginary crowd. Then he lowered his voice and looked almost beseechingly into her face, "And not as I decorated it for you."

Desdemona recoiled, knowing that it was the one thing that he feared and that yet must he tell her the one thing which would cause it, hoping against hope that she would somehow this time not react.

He lowered his eyes and continued as if submitting to

fate, whether good or bad, and yet sure that it would be bad, "They were not evil people. My master shared my work with me. My mother and I ate at his table with his family. He dressed us as he dressed his own children and in truth if I now think of my home and my family it is they that my heart turns to," and he paused a minute for this death-dealing information to sink into her heart, then continued in a rush of impetuosity, breathless to get the worst over, "But ever were I an ingrate, now I know it, ever were I rebellious, wild, and in truth I repaid him poorly," and his face was contrite with the thought of his adolescent crimes.

"Desdemona, it is gnawing at my bowels, I have never known rest from it except this one fatally peaceful moment with you and now my agony is redoubled so that I fear to lose my mind."

In exasperation she burst out, "But why should your youthful bad behaviour, if that it was, to a heathen and disbelieving people trouble you so dearest? It has only brought you good. It has brought you to the one true faith, for mysterious are the ways of the Lord." Desdemona betrayed ever so briefly the piety of the dried-out old ladies of Cyprus, the piety of those who, abandoned by faithless husbands for flighty young girls, sought refuge in lighting candles at the altars of saints this and that.

It was Otello's turn now to recoil at this unexpected glimpse of his beloved, a glimpse as it were of her true soul, which wounded him deeply. It was this insight that committed him now to take the plunge he had prevaricated over for so long, as it seemed to him the only conceivable course of salvation from the doom, he was ever more convinced with each advancing second, was due to fall on them both.

"I cannot, in all truth, see him as a heathen, Desdemona," he replied, allowing what he knew to be a bombshell to explode in the depths of their nocturnal discourse. She withdrew slightly from him, or rather without physically moving at all she shrank far away from him with all her being, like the tortoise which being tapped on the head retreats into its shell.

"Please believe me, I implore you, that I am only telling you this because I feel some impending doom which perhaps I can only avert if I am at last true, and if we face this together," and he was pleading with her now not to retreat from him at this moment into the iron shell of her faith, however comforting it might be for her on the troubled seas of her life, not to retreat into the armour plating that was her religion.

Otello, that miserable and doomed Moor, continued, "In truth, the Saracen lives his life more true to his faith than do we to ours," and then, deciding to take his compelling destiny in both his hands, he added, "And in truth, they live their lives more true to our faith, now I see it and confess it, than do we Christians."

Ripe with indignation she almost shouted, "The Saracen more true Christian than we! Now I adjudge you mad!" Desdemona's rage and scorn flushed her pale face and bosom lending her again a beauty even in her rejection. She snorted in barely controlled outrage, "Then why did you not become renegade, become Muslim, then why did you flee to us?"

"Folly! Only the youthful folly of an ingrate and a brute!" and the Moor shook his head in infinite regret at his own youthful impulses, "Sheer and utter folly. For all their kindness and goodness, something in me bade me reject them and strive with might and main to oppose them in anyway that I could. When my master, seeing that I had reached maturity, for the hairs had begun to sprout on my face, then my master who was the soul of decency took me aside and began to talk to me about Islam."

In a dreamlike state he began to remember that scene.

Sidi Ahmad, his master, had said, "I have never tried to force you to do the prayer, or to learn the practices of Islam as my own sons learn them Otello, because your mother is so much against it. Perhaps I am also too soft. But now we must talk because you are becoming a man and I fear for you, wild and headstrong youth that you are, if you do not know the truth."

Otello cried out to Desdemona, almost sobbing, "And do you know what I told him? That I would never become a Muslim but had decided to become a Christian and was determined to do so. Yet I told him that only because they were always at war only with the Christians, because I knew nothing about Christianity at all."

"But Otello, dearest, the Lord guided you even then," Desdemona interjected with all her fervent candle-lighting passion.

"Pshaw!" and he almost spat, "A young man's arrogance!"

Sidi Ahmad had said, "You can't be better followers of 'Isa, he whom they call Jesus, than are we. We follow his actual and real teachings while they have made a statue of him and nailed him to a wooden cross. They worship only pain and suffering. They only worship the thought that a man might become a god, which can never be, it is sheer folly and nonsense," and Sidi Ahmad had risen and left him in exasperation at his rebelliousness.

They had many conversations like that one and whatever Sidi Ahmad had offered of proof and reason, Otello had rejected out of hand, and all because he sided with his mother's equally stubborn refusal to submit. Yet he could never go back to her secret jiggery-pokery of African village life, practised under the bed-sheets without the knowledge of her masters, and so he chose the religion of the proud Venetian battleships.

Then with his mother's sudden death he had had nothing to hold him any longer and, partly unhinged with grief, he had escaped, killing whomever he could as if to punish them for her death, killing too his gentle master.

"But now I know Christianity, I have sat with the priests, with the most learned of them, learnt their dogmas and all the intricacies of the disputes of the theologians; I have prayed and fasted. All that can be said is that the Saracen is better than are we, better in his following Jesus, let alone Muhammad," he said it with a cool, clear detachment but yet with warmth and passion, and Desdemona shrank back even further from him, her bosom heaving noticeably. Evidently shocked as she was, yet she rallied somewhat so that Otello was caught unawares by her next words.

"What must we do, dear husband, now that we know this extraordinary truth?" and she presented a face transformed with concern and conviction, so convincing was it that he almost involuntarily answered her, "Long have I thought on that and of course realised that your people will never accept Islam, so we have no choice but to flee to the lands of the Muslims, secretly of course," simple-heartedly he told her.

She laughed, with the peels of laughter, which in any other circumstances he found winsome in the extreme, "Turn renegade? Me?" and he looked, shocked, at her face, realising only too late her momentary ruse.

Otello's heart sank, for such was his love for her and, if truth be told, for the position and honour he had attained, that he could perhaps no longer flee from the Christians as he had from the Saracen.

"If only she were to come with me …", but his sense of a doom pre-ordained settled on him and he resolved to close that door, never to return to the topic again. He rose as if to leave.

"Where are you going, dearest?" she asked, momentarily afraid that she had really hurt him with her laughter and that he was now seriously upset at her.

He smiled at her and banished heretical thoughts from his mind, dusting them under the great shadow which lurked there, accepting its doom, "I'm just going to see

my friend Iago, I have something to discuss with him,"
and he departed, leaving his shadow uneasily with her.

"Iago?" she muttered to herself, with mounting terror
as she heard his retreating footsteps and the slam of the
door, "Iago?" and then turned over and tried to sleep but
without success.

OISIN[1] SHEATHES
HIS SWORD

THE BETTER TO FIGHT

Oisin and Niamh[2]

OISIN dwelt in the land of men. He ran with the hounds, and the deer fell; great was their slaughter. Merry was the feasting of the Fian and their Fionn. Wild and exultant the revelry. Yet, sometimes, in their cups, was comrade transformed into foe over the champion's portion of meat, and head flew from shoulders.

Such was their life, between the merriment of the feast, the excitement of the chase and the fear and thrill of combat, war and death. Yet they had not been formed, this body of men, from mere folly; rather the lords and learned men of the Gael had farsightedly seen the very terrible threat from Roman legions poised on their borders and had formed the Fianna to face them. They had seen a great centralised empire sustained by ruthless

1   Pronounced 'O sheen'. In Scotland he is called Ossian.

2   Pronounced 'Neeve'.

military might, driven by the engine of usury to devour ever more lands and peoples. No freedom loving people would submit to that, without a fight. Thus the bodies of the Fianna had formed, the best of the youth of the Gael flocking to join under their banner.

Brave these Fianna and Fionn MacCumail[3], their chief, and Oisin the warrior-poet. In their lives too, dalliance with glorious women; in them too marriage and children.

Till Niamh came from the land of Tir na n-Og, the Land of Eternal Youth, beneath the Western Ocean.

It is little known that Niamh had come before that fateful day and since. Some she allowed a glimpse and they were ravished, distraught with an eternal sense of loss. Some were bitter that an unearthly beauty had laid waste to all lesser pursuits, and they found all pursuits to be lesser, to be nothing at all. Some were quietly transformed out of sheer gratitude at being allowed the grace of even a glance at such beauty once in their lives.

But to Oisin she came direct and called him with the tongue of love. Had he merely been a warrior he might from that call have killed Fionn and all the champions of the Fian for her. But, as he was poet, his tongue gave voice to every beautiful feeling in his breast, things he had never known till the moment he heard himself, as if another person, sing them out. So that he listened to his own song enrapt. He sang of things he had never known before and in the telling of which they proved eternally new, always replenished from hidden pools.

3   'Finn MacCool'.

Oisin then left the world of men, what we call history or the earth with all its combat and slaughter. Poet that he was, he went to dwell with her in her woman's world of Tir na n-Og which yet for all its magical lustre for him, had for Niamh herself been empty without man.

And Tir na n-Og, where is it but right here? Right beside us so to speak. Our people visit its lands and their people ours, but its eternal final door is death. Although near, its irrevocable rule is that it is not Earth and Earth is not it. And man while alive, for good or ill, is of Earth.

Yet, close as it is, to get there, they rode long on winged steeds to its door in the West beneath the ocean and there spent such time as they did.

Tir na n-Og is not in-time or out-of-time so that to say two hundred years or even a thousand is just a way of speaking. If it had been only half a minute still would Oisin have found on his return everything changed as if he had been gone a million years. For after Tir na n-Og nothing can ever be the same again.

Every leaf on every tree, every blade of grass, every human smile, each act of spontaneous kindness, each falling in love, each true song, is a miracle, each and every one. We are miracles surrounded by miracles. Merely cataloguing pedantically, detailing cause and effect, does not dispose of the sublime nature of life. So, what is a two-hundred year life in the scale of all-enveloping wonder?

As we have seen, a glance of the true Niamh, who can take the form of any woman if truth be told, takes any man instantly to Tir na n-Og if only for an instant. And what is an instant of eternity? How measure it?

Oisin dwelt there in rapture, pure and ineffable serenity, losing battle fever and blood lust as if they had never been. He was illumined there by the flowers and birds of Tir na n-Og and its people. They are indeed our flowers and birds and people, only seen and known with the eye and heart of the poet-lover.

How can I tell you? That land, which some have never smelt, and of which some had only a ravishing glimpse, Oisin dwelt in and came to know with the intimacy only possible to one who spends centuries of love and devotion. He knew each petal, was drunk on each leaf, branch and root. If that was the case, imagine then the ecstasy from discourse with refined and radiant beings, the illuminated people of Tir na n-Og. Imagine centuries of subtle and beautiful discourse on the secrets of 'is' and 'was' and 'ever shall be'. Then take from that a leap to the heights of the intimate exchange of secrets, glances and subtle fine thoughts with Niamh. For, with the men of Earth, love is the act of making love, but with the people of Tir na n-Og, that other-world, love finds its highest expression in stolen shy glances at the face of the beloved and in exchange of the knowledge of the beauty of a flower, and if love should be made then it is light upon light.

But pens are too coarse to write of it and words cannot even be used to hint at it. Whoever has known it knows what it means. Now know again that Oisin dwelt in that abode for centuries and then …

Then fools say he grew tired of it and longed for Earth.

Do you blame him, you who dwell on Earth longing for Heaven? Do you say within yourself, "I would not be that stupid, I would stay forever"? Do not be so sure. Indeed there are those who having glimpsed Tir na n-Og languish in yearning for it the rest of their lives and they are the majority. But Oisin had dwelt therein, had resided. He knew every brook and stream, every tree and flower, he knew its multitudinous folk. So well did he know it that he was finally certain that although he was of it and it of him, he also was of Earth. He pined then for Earth, they who do not understand say, for the hound's rending of the flesh of the deer, for that moment when the enemy's head flew from his shoulders. Yet it was not mere blood-lust that drew him back, for he did not go back; he went on.

Even if he had been in the Land of Youth for only the blinking of an eye he would have returned changed to a changed world; for if you change, the world is forever changed, utterly.

So, bravely he took his destiny in his hands, which was to go on, not back. He went on to whatever was his, good or ill. He had to be true to himself and his self was of Earth as much as of Heaven. Despite Niamh's sadness he went on to Earth.

Oisin and a Cleric

Having spent an eternity in youth, on coming to Earth he found himself to be old, very old. The heroes had gone, Fionn and his Fian, the Fianna Fail, the Warriors of Destiny, for they belong especially to youth. Instead he found the Adze-head, the Croziered one, a cleric of bells and vespers. In that meeting there is a clear ambivalence, for the warrior, poet and scholar, the lover who had known both the delights of Earth and Heaven and who had seized his destiny, bitter though it most definitely was, could recognise in the cleric's words certain truths, yet suspect that he himself knew more of those truths than the Adze-head.

There is a sense in which the cleric taught one he should have learnt from. He has embraced a doctrine of Heaven which he expounds to one only newly returned. Neither is he of Earth nor of Heaven, but a man of books, maps and doctrines. Oisin, for all his greatness of soul, confirms some of the doctrine while yet being sceptical of its propounder, sensing a certain lopsidedness of soul in him. Having come to Earth from Heaven, for a purpose and at a price, he tries to impart that knowledge to the cleric who only sees in him a yearning for the wicked old days of paganism. Moreover, Oisin senses that, perhaps wittingly but almost certainly unwittingly, the cleric is an agent of that great imperial force which it is the very essence of Oisin's being to fight.

So, Oisin returned to Earth, while not returning, to fulfil his destiny, if only that he had to be buried in it. Yet, great soul that he was, he could not even totally die, his story was not over, his destiny not quite fulfilled. Rather than fulfilment he sensed the cleric as an inappropriate punctuation mark, a comma rather than the full-stop that marks a sentence completely said and done with. More seriously, he realised that although the cleric did not know it, he was the means of the Roman invasion and colonisation of the Gaels, an invasion which might never have been done by military means but was quietly and effectively done by religious invasion.

Oisin did not find the heroes that he returned in longing for, not Fionn nor his Fianna. He did find a cleric and a band of followers.

The distress he endured cannot be exaggerated, for when age comes on a man all of a sudden it is no small affair, and age comes always all of a sudden, overnight as it were.

It is well known, this encounter of aged warrior-poet, splendid pagan as he is portrayed, and the modern ascetic cleric; of how the cleric, despite his disapprobation of Oisin's pagan values, yet basks in his tales of the hunt and the battle. But much has been left out of these accounts, since they were written by that cleric and transmitted by his own ilk whose partiality and bias are not in dispute.

The encounter is not merely that of a primitive with a harbinger of the modern. That Oisin was not schooled in Aristotle's metaphysics did not prevent him from having direct access to genuinely metaphysical dimensions of existence, and I mean, Tir na n-Og. The cleric for his part had not even smelt its fragrance but he could read maps which located it precisely.

"Tell me, brave Oisin, of Fionn and his wonderful

exploits," that cleric began his questioning as was his habit one night as they sat around a campfire. They were on one of the cleric's missionary peregrinations.

"Perish the thought, cleric," spoke Oisin, "that I should tell to the agent of empire the adventures of that man whose mission was to protect the Gael from her."

"But Oisin, dear pulse, barbaric Rome has gone; the new gospel has all but vanquished her," the cleric replied, astonished yet again at the vehemence of Oisin's feelings.

"Far from it! I recognise all to clearly that old Rome has merely changed her imperial garb," Oisin spat out passionately, "and most likely will change dress more times too in years to come."

"Ah, old pagan yet; accept the gospel; believe in ..." and the cleric began to rapture effusively until Oisin cut him short.

"That gospel I have accepted, as you well know, which accords well with what I know, but as for that hocus-pocus of three-in-one and one-in-three, bread into meat, human meat, and wine into blood, human blood, human god meat and blood, whether real or metaphorical, I'll have none of it," and he spat in disgust.

The cleric recoiled and a few of his fellow monks could be seen reaching for weapons; heroes they might not be, but the fighting, quarrelling Gael lay not far from the surface in any one of them.

The cleric stood and stepped back with his arms out as if to stem the great tide of armed monks about to descend with slaughter on the aged hero. They in turn pressed on his arms as if straining to get at Oisin. Oisin, though aged, knew himself able to inflict some harm yet and indeed cared no more now than when young for death, feared it little, whereas these monks yet shook at the thought of it. An uneasy stillness followed as all resumed their seats sullenly.

"Cleric, O cleric, my people, as you know, are much given to story and tale, but never despise the tale, for by it many a great truth has been told to hearts that can know it, and yet many a lie too for hearts asleep and undiscerning," began Oisin. He paused briefly, for he felt the ocean a-tremble upon his tongue, perhaps the very ocean beneath which lay Tir na n-Og, and he hesitated before the great outpouring of his heart's oceanic truths.

"Cleric, O cleric, you have brought me two bags. In one bag is that great treasure of truths from that noble Galilean which accords well with the very best the wise and holy ones of my people have taught. But the other bag is this tale, this curious myth which I have exercised all my poet's craft and druid wisdom in disentangling, and having done so I am appalled!"

The cleric blanched deeply, not because he had understood the import of Oisin's words, but because the very truthfulness of the man carried a weight which was almost physical like the punch of a mailed fist or the slice of a great double-handed sword.

"Beware Oisin, great-limbed heathen," the cleric tremblingly began, rage threatening to carry off the last vestiges of his sanctity. Greatly resentful was he that this once-mighty, now feeble old man could still so discomfit him, "beware of …"

But Oisin's rage was different, for he was master of it, not it of him, and he was astride it now with a great-hearted battle-axe aloft.

"Woe to you cleric! Listen to my tale! Rather, listen to your tale as I now see it so clearly." Then as if recollecting something he turned and addressed the monks, and said to them, "and you Gaels, grandsons and granddaughters of Eireann, brothers and sisters of Scotia listen to me."

What a strange group then it was that camped that night in the forest, (for that was a time when the lands of the Gael still had forests). How many different thoughts those hearts brought to hearing wild Oisin and his deciphering of the Christian tale. The cleric only saw his mission, his role as a leader of men, as one of those who are entered in history's scrolls as one of the elect. As for the monks, among them were those who were in fear and trembling as to the eternal damnation or salvation of their souls, and such as these were inwardly withdrawn like the inhabitants of a besieged city who only wait for the encamped enemy to depart and who yet stand eagerly on the battlements scrutinising every detail of the enemy. Others had joined the little group of eager monks because, for various reasons, they had found themselves on the outside of clan power structures when they desperately wanted to be on the inside or at the top. Others had been enthralled by the wisdom contained in the first bag Oisin had described, the beautiful, fearful challenging wisdom of the Galilean, and they had not discerned that with it came the second alien bag. This group of pure-hearted ones were already torn between conflicting loyalties, for the noble eloquent old warrior rang true in their very bones in a way that this Romanised Celtic cleric did not, and probably never could.

"O cleric, my cleric, our people know many a tale, many a grand romance, of heroes who were noble, brave and fearless in battle, soft, tender and caring in love, generous to friend and foe alike. Though there be somewhat in them of exaggeration, yet they engender in the hearts of those snared by them, at the very least, love of nobility, generosity, magnanimity and all the fine qualities of man and woman." And Oisin looked intently out of his feeble rheumy eyes forcibly and directly at his audience, one by one, to see were they with him on the journey he was taking. "And I dread lest there come a time when men will tell tales of the ignoble, bestial, mean and hardhearted so that people who hear them incline to them and the people go to ruin entirely."

Despite themselves the spellbound monks paled in horror at the glimpse afforded them of some perhaps not-so-remote depravity of the human race.

"Now this tale, Adze-head, O you of the crozier and the vespers, this tale of yours, which you have unwrapped from this second bag of yours, let me see how I can truly decipher it to you, for I see that you yourself have not truly grasped its import," and Oisin looked with such a mixture of ferocity and genuine kindliness at the cleric that he felt himself to have been both slapped and embraced at the same moment, an experience so confusing to him that he, who was almost never lost for words despite his all-too frequent deprecation of his lack of learning, was now utterly silent.

"O my tender priest, my little chanter of psalms and mumbler of prayers, I feel your heart a good one. What I say is to deliver you, as it were, from the mouth of a tremendous dragon which is about to devour you and through you the rest of the Gaels," and Oisin called out, magnificent warrior that he was, to his cleric, from strength, not weakness, like the great fighter who begs the callow youth not to fight him, knowing beyond doubt that he will absolutely slaughter him. It was this then that called up the ancient battle urge in the cleric, for he would not be condescended to.

"Tell us your tale, Oisin," the cleric said, "for though we had thought you would amuse us with tales of old Fionn and his sturdy Fianna, yet if you will not, then amuse us as you will."

The glint in the cleric's eyes told Oisin that the lines were drawn for battle indeed, and so he drew in his breath, a feeble breath of an exhausted body and prepared for what might be his last and infinitely most important battle.

"O Adze-head, there is a tale now told about a great and noble man, a godly man though not a god, that as I see claims to honour that man but has betrayed him," and the monks shifted uneasily in the light of their campfire, not quite sure of where this tale would go. "Now I say that this man was a real and true man, a great man and yet this tale told of him a lie, a monstrous lie."

Oisin fell into deep thought as he struggled in his old poet's heart for how this story must be allowed to tell itself to reach these other hearts.

"There is a word I need, for I would not talk of Rome; it is not about Rome I really speak. Perhaps you can help me, you tonsured ones, you book-readers, to find that word, for I know it not. What is it that Rome is, or Pharaoh's Egypt or Darius' Persia?"

"They are kingdoms," ventured one monk.

"Right you are," spoke Oisin, "but it is not that I seek, for kings and their kingdoms we know; they come and go. We Gaels know them, and they are of no matter, for these I have mentioned go beyond kingdoms greatly."

"They are empires," said another, more learned in the wider world and its affairs.

"That is true too," said Oisin, "but it is not yet that I seek though it is undoubtedly further along the road to it, for what are empires but great kingdoms that swallow up lesser kingdoms for a season or two, and then they too go their way."

"I have heard people," said another, "and they, when talking of these matters, would talk always of the 'state'."

"It is a word I know not fully, brother," said Oisin eagerly, "but something in me tells me that this is indeed the very word. So I will tell my tale using this word and you, who are more learned than am I, will tell me if it fits as I use it," and the monks, who were now eagerly attentive, nodded in agreement and waited for the tale.

"We return to the noble godly man I mentioned. Tender monks, he was of a people not unlike our Gaelic people but more like the people of this Briton," and he gestured, not hostilely, towards the cleric. "Now ask me in what lies the resemblance to us which is yet more of a resemblance to the Britons."

The monks looked to each other and to the cleric who was as unengaged in this singularly Gaelic story event as were they engaged. So, by means of that mastering communal intuition everywhere apparent in human groupings, they spontaneously elected another spokesman, and they elected him by nothing so vulgar as the raising of an eyebrow, and that man, Fergus, spoke for them. "In what does that resemblance lie, brave Oisin?" asked Fergus.

Oisin smiled to his people and said, "It lies, O monk, in that, like us and like the Britons, this noble man's people had been a free people under their own kings and with godly inspired men living among them, celebrating the rituals that please the great God. They lived in harmony with the spirit of things and then, let us say, they began to forget," and he imparted to that seemingly unimportant word "forget" a significance that made it hover around the campfire like a terrible Banshee of doom. For what doom is not concealed in forgetting and what victory not heralded by remembrance?

"They forgot first the honour due the noble man, be he

sage or hero, or be he king, and when they did that then they belied them, some they dishonoured, and some they even killed. And then the 'state' came with its legions, its record-keepers, its tax-gatherers, its slave labour, and its priests, several times in their history, and the last time it came as Rome. In that way, these people resemble our Britons across the sea," and he leant a little closer to them, looking into their faces through the flickering light of the fire.

"Here we have this people and a state, kingdom or empire—call it what you will—and we have this godly man," Oisin continued.

The cleric looked as if he were about to interrupt and Oisin snapped out at him, as if he had read his mind, "A godly man, I say, cleric, not a god-man," and the cleric backed, backed away from whatever he had meant to say.

"This man will be a model for many who come after and maybe for many people for aeons to come after us; who knows? So let us examine this myth that has been foisted on him, cleric; let you and I without prejudice examine that myth, or at least this one part. For cleric, I'll make so bold as to assert that this crucifixion part of the myth is the damnedest lie and the biggest disaster ever to come upon the human race."

The monks were thrown into consternation at this forthright statement of his case but the cleric was as if pleased to have his opponent openly confess to being the grandest heretic ever to grace a discussion.

"How can you say such a thing, Oisin?" exclaimed one of the monks, "when it is the very pivot of our faith, which you yourself have accepted?"

"Not so the pivot, my heart," replied Oisin. "That pivot is the life and teaching of this great and wise-hearted man, and it is that I have embraced so much as I am able."

Fergus here, "And we have heard from some of the ancient rites in the East, that someone who resembled our Lord was put in his place. It was adjudged heresy, it is true. But for now, let us hear this great pagan out."

With trepidation each sat with his thoughts, some worrying at the threat to their faith, others at the threat to their position, and Oisin as to whether he could say what he had to say not only truly but well, for to speak truly is given to many as is to speak well, but to speak truly and well is given to a very few.

"There are many things in the false myth I could speak of, things which directly contradict the real teaching, the actual life and words of that great being but it is only one thing I want to speak about now, for I grow old and tired and must make my words count lest they be my last," he said, and paused again before resuming. "The noblest of men the world has yet seen is made by a myth-maker, tale-teller to submit himself to the most ghastly humiliation of a death at the hands of the 'state', and it is declared to be his highest destiny, and in that he will be the model for generations, for aeons to come afterwards. Thus that 'state' keeps growing. I fear that it will come to cover the whole earth as the best of men offer themselves up to be crucified in deluded emulation of him, rather than in fighting to see that justice and the law are preserved. They surrender in suffering with the deluded and sick desire of becoming God. What delusion is worse than that, tell me, monks? For God ever *is*. All that the noble and wise have ever said is that the Lord is the Lord and the slave is the slave. This delusion is your religion. It is the left hand of an empire whose right hand is legions, might and power."

In the sallow light of the dying embers of the fire, he looked into their eyes, one by one, and saw that all but one of them had recognised to different degrees what he said. Some were, however, resignedly and fatalistically going to their slaughter under the compelling hypnosis of that myth. The cleric, Oisin could not see into his now deeply cold eyes. "And you," thought Oisin, "are more crucifying than crucified."

Then, deeply exhausted, he went to lay himself down on some animal skins to sleep. When the monks sought him in the morning they found he had died in the night. His face bore the look of a man who had rejoined his Niamh or perhaps his beloved Fionn and the Fianna.

Another man, even as Oisin took his tired body to rest, sleep and death, had sat quietly alone late into the night, electrified, unable to sleep, in a mixture of terror and excitement. When the monks sought him in the morning, Fergus too was gone.

Oisin Waits Even Now

They say that ghosts are people who die in some fashion

such that they don't realise that they have died and so wander the earth, puzzled at their encounters with its denizens. Perhaps also, some ghosts are those spirits who have not fully lived and so cannot fully die.

Oisin, great heart, could not fully die with the jigsaw puzzle of his life incomplete with the oddly fitting Adze-head piece, both an emissary of true revelation much in harmony with the Gael's Druidic teaching and an agent for the forces of empire and state. A picture there was but something wrong, very wrong about it.

He did die but his ghost lived on in ever greater puzzlement at the course of the cleric's story and what he bequeathed to the Gael.

At first the spirit of Oisin almost thought that he had misjudged the cleric, for his teaching set fire to the Gaelic imagination in a way that gladdened the old warrior druid, not least with the life of indomitable Colmcille, Columba of Iona. Here was warrior and king, druid and poet all in one figure; here was a man.

At this critical time, as the tide of Colmcille's teaching became full and began to ebb, and the great and awful, that strange empire-church reached out and tried to snuff out whatever light they'd lit, those Gaels, at that point Oisin saw it and knew it. He wanted to cry out, "Look, Gaels, look over there, at the very centre of the earth's lands!" He saw godly warriors, wild and good, he saw men and women, whose prayers and battles had the same intensity, whose living and dying were suffused with Tir na n-Og.

He saw a man whom the one the cleric followed resembled, who knew the sanctity of prayer, giving and fasting, whose words were concise but full of wisdom, who fed the hungry and gave them to drink when there was little or no food or water, but who also knew the family home, women and children, who was husband, lover and father. He knew the marketplace well and warned them against usury and corrupt commercial practices. He had a law, a law, moreover, not unlike the Gael's Brehon law. And he was a guide leading them on in their spiritual development. This man was valiant, none more so, on the battlefield, yet leading his warriors in prayer in the midst of battle, for nothing was more important to them than their Lord. They were on a Way.

Then Oisin saw two great bestial tyrant empires reel before the onslaught of these saintly wild people. He saw that they did not fight for conquest, but for justice on the earth and God's law and so they won and conquered. He sensed that the cleric's age was over. "Look Gaels, look over there; they are like us; they are more like us," he tried to cry out. But, alas, they were too far away; the Gaels could not see them nor could they hear Oisin calling out from the unseen.

The cleric's legacy proved more tenacious than he had thought. In his disappointment then, it was almost with relish that he saw the long-limbed blond Norsemen and Danes come, sturdy sailors, intense farmers, traders and such warriors as he would have loved to meet in battle – fine, fine enemies. It was with regret that he saw them take the cleric's path and the light go out from their warrior eyes.

Then there came those other Norsemen, the Normans, more calculating by far, with the fight of the Vikings and yet the organisation that is the 'state'. But these, like the Vikings, had married the women and become more Gaelic than the Gael, these Butlers, Fitzgeralds and noble Bruces.

Oisin had watched in apprehension as the land of the Britons, which alone of the British Celts had felt the brute force of the legions, became, as it were, the anvil upon which some terrible weapon is forged into shape. He saw with horror the old dream of empire glitter madly in monarchs' eyes and he saw moneylenders standing eager to fit out every army at kings' bchests with the blessing of mother church.

Oh yes, there were ever outbursts of that Gaelic quarrelsomeness and rebellion to gladden his heart, not least when some even of the clerics, Luther, Calvin and Knox, threw off the outward shackles of the empire-church. "But if you don't get rid of the inward shackles and chains, someone will come and tie you up again," he wanted to shout to them, and then the two parties fell on each other in a bitter struggle that was to last centuries, divide the Gaels inextricably in two, and allow the enemy to establish his power. The cleric's divided followers fought each other, totally ignoring the wrong around them. In that struggle the Bank was born with the connivance of those clerics and Oisin wept for the Gaels, truly.

Defeat followed defeat, and then there was humiliation and worse. They were cleared from their land and sent around the world to serve as the lowest of slaves, if they survived the journeys. Or they were enrolled as the backbone of an empire's armies, only to return home from faraway wars to find themselves and their families long evicted from their homes by that same empire-state.

Yet it was clear to Oisin that now their suffering was only one suffering among many as the world's peoples came under the sway of states run by banks which were ever so gradually but surely becoming one super-state.

Perhaps worst of all was to see a part of the Gaels, among a multitude of others, bravely fighting and winning, only for them then to form a little state and enforce on themselves every measure they had fought centuries to be rid of. That they did, after falling upon each other in the most awful fratricidal war. Most vexatious to his troubled spirit was it to see a portion of the Gaelic peoples granted a nationhood which marked ironically and quite cynically their complete subjugation to control, a subjugation at which they themselves connived thinking it to be their liberation.

If passion alone and indignation could have restored life to his rotting limbs, Oisin would have risen from the grave and dragged Fionn and all out with him to combat the mounting humiliation of the Gaels and all the small nations, but that was not to be. The old spirit leapt with excitement at those moments when the Gael threw off vestments, mitres and croziers, and took to gun, sword and cannon. Yet these too were incomplete and puzzling.

If the centuries in Tir na n-Og were just the blinking of an eye, this nigh on two millenniums weighed heavily on Oisin's spirit and seemed to drag with a sort of tedium, enlivened only by the not infrequent outbreaks of wildness and rebellion. "A grey age," he thought with a sort of revulsion at such constriction of the human spirit. The grey obscuring mist spread across the planet eclipsing the lights of all the little nations and merging them into one protoplasmic political blob.

Yet Oisin stood and waited, his sword at the ready, sure yet that he would see the Divine spark ignite his people. And he has seen that this age is a different age, its combats more ambiguous, more treacherous. He saw the tremendous slaughter across the earth, men, women and children obliterated by machines and bombs. He has seen the madness that is in the warriors who kill the ordinary folk for no reason, and so he saw the need to sheathe the sword thoughtfully, not in defeat but the better to fight. He knows now that the age of the cleric has finally come to a close; it has exhausted itself totally, and used up every resource and trick at its disposal.

Oisin awaits now the coming of the Way to his people. He knows it has the bravery of the Fianna, the excitement of the chase of the hounds after the wild, wild boar, the fierceness of battles in it, and the sweetness of women in it. It is of Earth. There is tenderness, there is playfulness of children. There is the encounter with the majesty and beauty of the Divine and with the ethereal other of Tir na n-Og. There too is teaching, the Book that encompasses all extremes and opposites as does the Way itself, both Law and Revelation of the Unseen. There is in it the restoration of market places and the freedom of people to go and sell there without rents, taxes or any control. There is the abolition of states and taxes. There are in it peoples, clans, and Fianna of warriors of truth, gentle and chivalrous to women, capable of great love, and of death-dealing blows where needed, for without them the great grey death will stifle the life of the earth. He knows that it is for all the peoples, the little and the great nations under the burden of the great taxing policing super-state, and that if the Chechens, the Basques and the multitudinous little tribal nations of South America are not free, then the Gaels won't be free either.

Oisin waits. He knows it must come. He stands in Tir na n-Og, with his sword sheathed but ready, Fionn, the Fianna and Niamh at his side.

THE GREATEST NAME OF ALLAH

The story is told of how a young Muslim seeker of knowledge came to the Shaykh Dhu'n-Nun al-Misri in Cairo and spent many years with him, yet without the opening of his inner eye. Thus as a middle aged man one day he approached Dhu'n-Nun and asked him to teach him the Supreme Name of Allah, al-Ism al-cAdham, by which if Allah is called He answers and if He is begged He gives. Dhu'n-Nun told him that he was unable to teach him it but that he would send him to a man who lived on an island on the Nile who could teach it to him. He entrusted his pupil with a box containing a present for the man and told him to convey his greetings.

The pupil set off then till he came to the Nile where he hired a boat and began to row towards the island. He was distracted in his rowing by the occasional rustling and scratching noise issuing from the box. Finally, unable to restrain his curiosity further, he shipped his oars, picked up the box and looked inside. A rather frightened mouse blinked back at him and then suddenly leaped from the box into the boat. The man scrambled after it and the mouse, eager to escape, leaped into the Nile and quickly disappeared from sight.

The man, rather puzzled, resumed his rowing and soon the island came in view. The teacher was standing on its shore as if expecting him. He greeted him, conveyed Dhu'n-Nun's greetings and explained the purpose of his visit. The teacher made him welcome, showed him every hospitality and then enquired, "Perhaps Dhu'n-Nun sent you with something for me? That has been his custom."

"Yes indeed," the student replied embarrassedly, "He asked me to bring you this box," and he presented it to him.

The teacher took it, looked inside and remarked, "But this box is empty!?" so that the student, even more embarrassedly, replied, "Yes it is," and explained the whole story of the mouse.

"Do you mean to say," asked the teacher, "That you cannot bring me one mouse with which you have been entrusted safely and you expect me to teach you the Greatest Name of Allah!?" He said it with such passion and vigour that the student crumbled and wept at the realisation of his plight. He humbly begged the man to forgive him, but he was unrelenting until, finally, after much contrition on the pupil's part, he said, "There is a way for you. I will not teach you the Greatest Name of Allah but there is a way. You must take yourself to one of the remotest border lands of the Muslims, find a town with a mosque in it and you must teach there every day. Mind you, every day!"

The student submitted then and thanked the teacher and returned to Cairo. He lost no time in finding Dhu'n-Nun, telling him all that had happened, taking leave of him and setting out on the journey that was to be his life.

He crossed through the Sinai desert, through Sham which is now Palestine, Syria and Lebanon, on through Asia Minor and on further into the vast Asiatic regions. There in the mountains he came across a particular town about which he had an intuition and entering its mosque he sat down and taught. This he did every day. At first only one or two sat with this curious stranger from far away. Then gradually the circle increased until, as years passed, it reached to become a great circle of students.

Yet, the town already had a number of scholars who became jealous at the increase of his circle. After some years when his circle was at its greatest extent they began a campaign against him alleging that his path was not orthodox, that it was heretical. At first this campaign had no effect at all. Yet over the years it began slowly to detach some of the least firmly grounded so that the circle decreased ever so slightly.

With the years that almost imperceptible change began to gather momentum until, after many more years had passed, it reached the point that one day only three of the strongest pupils remained. Then one day only two came to his class. One of the two was so agitated that suddenly, covered with confusion, he got up while his master was talking and, without explanation, left the mosque. The master looked at the one remaining student who was unable to return his gaze and finally left the mosque too.

The strain of these years had told and the now-aged teacher broke down and wept, for he had not yet reached to the knowledge of the Greatest Name of Allah. At that moment a woman of just the sort known to the world as Dervish entered the mosque. She had a staff and a bag which contained the little she needed during her travels. She stamped her staff loudly on the mosque floor to catch the weeping man's attention and then said to him vehemently, "Did he not say, 'Every day'? Did he not say, 'Every day' ?"

The old man watched through his tears as she left and then, pulling himself together, continued his lesson to the now empty mosque. Each day at the same time he taught the empty mosque. The townsfolk came and went. They overheard snatches, tantalising snatches, but it was only after years that first one or two and then increasing numbers of people began to return to his class, to the circle to which the Shaykh now taught the Greatest Name of Allah.

* * *

There are elements in this story which merit study over and above the deep wisdom in its basic tale. What is referred to as the Greatest Name of Allah could be taken for now as a symbol of that knowledge whereby the heart of a man takes wings and flies. How different it is from the drear repetition of facts and data, cases and conclusions, which scholars of every age are prone to indulge in – the Islamic 'Alim no less than the statistician or the geneticist. So, without probing too far for now into the exact meaning of this element which is not the purpose of our enquiry, let us accept it as a symbol of the desire to swim in the depths of the ocean of knowledge rather than take buckets of data out of it.

The student had spent twenty years with Dhu'n-Nun and he had not plumbed the depths nor flown. What was he studying? Let us look for that to the figure of Dhu'n-Nun. A quite historical figure buried now in a known but neglected grave in Cairo's City of the Dead. The first encounter with Dhu'n-Nun gives one the immediate impression of "Yes, here is one who has flown, here is one who has plumbed the depths." He is from a very early generation of Muslims indeed. Statements he makes are very challenging and so he is taken before the Khalifah to be questioned on his orthodoxy. Rumours, wild rumours have obviously reached the Khalifah but when he meets the man and talks with him it is clear that this man is a Muslim.

Dhu'n-Nun is of a very early generation and those early generations are of great interest to us. Despite all our best efforts they are men and women who cannot be pigeon-holed. We hear of a man who is a great jurist, a legist, a lawyer and what not – and there you have him standing each night through in prayer, weeping before Allah. Equally the saintly spiritual ones who have been co-opted by the contemplatives of later generations to their causes can be found deeply embroiled in the issues, the jihads of their day.

Dhu'n-Nun, we come across him entirely by accident it seems, in a long list of people who narrated the Muwatta from Malik. It is very easy to pass over that statement in a facile manner, so let us look deeper at what we know about that.

Malik is Madinah. He recognised the significance of Madinah and he documented it. He recognised that the Messenger of Allah, may Allah bless him and grant him peace, had created a Madinah Munawwarah – an Illuminated City – a city of illuminated beings and that that city had endured down to his third generation and so he wrote it down. He wrote it down so that whoever wished to preserve the illuminated city could, and whoever wished to create a new illuminated city or cities would have a model of the best to work from. In that primal model, form and content are inextricably united – practice and illumination are one.

When a man said to Malik, "I want to learn from you," Malik replied, "Then take up residence." He did not encourage the study of texts in a library, university or even madrasah. His subject was Madinah and the proper place for its study was Madinah. Malik had, in this way, an astonishing number of pupils from all over the earth, east and west. They all knew that the Messenger of Allah, may Allah bless him and grant him peace, loved the people of Madinah, had taught them, had illuminated them, had told them to stay together and not leave the Madinah and that they had obeyed him, preserved his knowledge and transmitted it faithfully. Their greatest transmission had been in their living it daily in Madinah.

This was what Dhu'n-Nun imbibed. Dhu'n-Nun narrated the Muwatta from memory. He shows few other signs of being one of those memorisers of dusty texts so this text must have held a high place in his heart for him to have memorised it.

Dhu'n-Nun's image comes down to us over the ages as an ecstatic, a spiritually drunken man. We live in a rather trivial age that sees everything in splits and oppositions – he was a spiritual man so he could not have been a formal legal man – and yet here we have Dhu'n-Nun narrating Muwatta from memory. It is not just an accidental fact or a curiosity of his biography. He was not ecstatic in spite of this but because of it, because he had drunk deep of the knowledge of the illuminated city he was illuminated, luminous, he was drunk, he had a heart which plumbed the depths of the oceans.

His student spent twenty years with him. What was he doing? Of course he was learning this matter but a block remained. He was not living it. His living of it was to share it, transmit it, teach it to others. He would know what it truly was if he taught it but because he just had it he couldn't be it. That he himself conceptualised his dilemma as his need of a special invocation, a dhikr, a secret name of Allah which would bestow knowledge on him was his confusion. But he knew already. For him to know his own knowledge there only remained for him to teach it. There remained only for him to find a Madinah and transmit the light of the illuminated city for he himself to be illuminated. He thought of it as the matter of his own illumination. The reality is that it is a social matter. If the polis is illuminated then each one, each individual will be illuminated. An essential part of the illuminated nature of that city was the sharing of the people, their almost total sharing of the highest and least of life, their abandonment of seeking their own mere advantage, their seeing their own good as lying in the welfare of their neighbours, their townsfolk.

The student's life quest was to become such a Madinan man and thus illuminated. And yet because it is his own quest for light, at the pivotal moment he must go on whether the Madinah will or no. With such people a single man transforms a city but the city is incapable of transforming a single man.

Makkah, Dhu'l-Hijjah 1413

POETRY

GOD IS DEAD

WHO KILLED HIM?
    We did!
    We located Him
    and confined Him to the heavens,
    excluding Him from the earth,
We dared to make images of Him.
We gave the Ancient of Days
        a long grey beard
        and a human form.
We cast His role
        as lying at the beginning of creation,
        with odd interventions
        here and there in history.
We only conceded to Him "Acts of God"
        strange capricious disasters
        which insurance companies
        will not cover.
We restricted His worship to drafty,
        old, stone buildings,
        one day out of seven.
We gave Him Who has no form as we know it,
        a human form,
        and when a mortal human being

> reminded us of God's transcendence
> we elevated that man into a deity.
Our scientists stole His laws,
> straight plagiarism.
> The planets had moved in elliptical orbits
> for millions of years
> before Newton 'discovered'
> the Laws of Motion.
Lacking a Supreme Being we elevated nature
> to a position not hers.
> Then we methodically set out
> to conquer this power,
> devastating land,
> sea, our food
> and the very air we breathe.
Already satisfied that we had got rid of God,
> we revived an assembly of lesser gods
> that would have confused the Greeks,
> embarrassed the Romans
> and are the envy of the Hindus.
We are contemptuous of worship and prayer,
> yet we pass our lives
> in a thousand empty rituals,
> adoring and propitiating
> a multitude of friendly
> and hostile gods.
We spend lives dedicated to eating and drinking.
> Is this not worship?
We have committed ourselves

to spending the greater part of our lives
making money,
and by that we make money our god,
for no ascetic monk in his little cell
ever showed more complete devotion.
We have restored the old idol
of voluptuous sexuality,
and its nubile form graces our newspapers,
films, our walls
and our dreams.
It, in its turn, has rewarded us
with venereal diseases,
their sister AIDS
and social disintegration
on an unparalleled scale.
We are too proud to bow before God,
but we will crawl on our faces
to the bank manager,
when we run into trouble on our mortgages.
We are, in fact, living our lives
in order to buy our houses,
like Pharaoh
who dedicated his reign
to building his pyramidical tomb.
With God passed away Heaven and Hell
and in their place we put the fantasy,
never-never land
of computer graphics
and its fully-automated,

> centrally-heated,
> double-glazed,
> fast-food brothel
> which has unfortunately
> the terrifying potential
> to metamorphose
> into the Gulag Archipelago,
> genocidal massacres and state tyranny
> as a way of life.

So God is dead.
We killed Him.
Yet the God we killed does not exist anyway.

> God one-of-three
> does not exist.
> God old man with grey beard
> does not exist.
> God remote above the heavens
> does not exist.
> God of this or that people
> does not exist.
> God who sent His son
> does not exist.

There is no god,
But Allah.
Allah is One.

> He is not located in any place,
> for if He were,
> He would be limited and so,
> not divine.

He has no form,
> for He is the ceaseless originator of all forms.
He eternally creates the entire cosmos,
> and He sustains every photon,
> atom, cell
> and quasi-stellar object
> at every instant.
> Without Allah they do not exist.
He sustains every living thing,
> Christian, Jew, Hindu or Atheist.
He is not the Lord of the Arabs,
> or the Jews,
> or the Christians,
> but Lord of the Worlds,
> of all beings
> and of all Being.
No thing resembles Him,
> no image nor concept,
> yet He is the Hearing, the Seeing.
He has no son,
> for His son would have to be a god
> with limitless power
> and it is impossible
> for two omnipotent beings to exist,
> they would limit each other.
> Anything limited is not a god.
He has terrible might and power,
> and sublime mercy and compassion.
He is far exalted above

being one out of a pair of opposites.
He is Allah.
>He is the Answerer.
>He is the Vast.
>He is the Universally Merciful.
God is dead.
Allah *is*,
The Living Who does not die.

THE COLT

A colt first saddled bolts,
    – the connection more than rhyme
    it's what it does, it's what it is,
a bolt from out of time.

Yet it can learn to stand,
under unflinching stare,
roar of traffic and, in ages past,
rage of battle and war.

Why not then endure
   the Master's gaze,
     of kindly expert care?
Why shy away
   from other colts?
     why that startled stare?

Much as it loves freedom,
much as it loathes the saddle,
it clearly has a purpose,
it knows it's made for travel.

Brave colt be still,
    be calm,
        you're safe.
The caravan's
    the company,
The caravan's
    the place.

The cavalry,
    the cavalcade,
The caravan's
    the place.
Only in the company,
you'll find your proper space.

Outwith the orchestra,
the violin's a screech,
outwith the caravan,
the colt's still in breech,
in breech of law and custom,
flaunting way and goal,
come back, dear colt, and travel on,
or else remain a foal.

Who loves the goal,
so loves its people,
for love's the goal,
love is the people.

Love's the journey,
and the journeying,
the wayfarer,
and wayfaring.

What better goal?
What other way?
What other company!
Colt! do stay.

Stay the course,
the goal is clear,
colt, don't bolt,
don't fear.

❉ ❉ ❉

And, dear soul,
    if you see me flee
then say a
    prayer for me.

Likewise a fall,
    a swerve,
        a slip,
how else
        could it be?

My slip's yours, your swerving mine,

the caravan's unbending rule.
We're all together on this way,
until we reach the goal.

Whose eye is on the goal,
has no time for others' slips;
whose heart is on the way,
can see no other failings
than his own.

For we are mirrors,
    to each other;
we are brothers,
    to one another.

***

And if my own self's the colt,
what then? I hear you say.
What refuge from its waywardness?
What solace for me? You say.

If it's my own self that bolts,
you the mirror of it,
what then you say? Indeed, what then?
For you and me and it?

Then, I beg you,
    kindly caravan,

        cavalcade
            of brothers dear,
O'erlook my slip,
    catch me when I fall.
        Without you,
            life is drear.

I say to myself
    what I say to you,
O wayward
    dashing youth,
take heed my words,
may they take you to the truth:

While we travel on,
what matters is the bond
that ties each one to other,
each man to each other brother,
each woman sister, mother,
    daughter, wife.
a community, a society, a life.

And a colt once saddled yields,
it knows it's destiny.
Its fate it trusts. Its fate to reach,
it must ride in company.